SUMMER AND SHINER

WINNER OF THE 1992 HEARTH AWARD

BY
NOLAN CARLSON
Dedicated to Wholesome Literature for Young Adults

Hearth
PUBLISHING

A Division of Multi Business Press
Hillsboro, KS

Summer and Shiner
Copyright© 1992 by Hearth Publishing

First Edition
Printed in the USA
by Multi Business Press

Cover Illustration: Chris Andrade
Story Illustrations: Fred Carlson

ISBN: 0-9627947-4-0
Library of Congress No. 92-71256

To my son, Jason,
and to the students at Central Elementary

SUMMER AND SHINER
by Nolan Carlson

I like to smell that strong catfish smell of the Blue River while I'm sitting and watching the yellow moon light up the slow-moving water. A body can sit there in the evening listening to the frogs croak and mosquitoes whine around his head and watch the blue fog settle in, coating the Flint Hills. It's great when you got nothing else to do. And it's free, besides.

Back in the late 1940's, my folks were poor. Oh, we're not dirt poor: My dad is a small town grocer who does his best for his family. He isn't a real big man, but he's got a mighty big heart. There's always some poor widow getting an extra two or three ounces of summer sausage without paying for it.

A whole lot of farmers have to charge their groceries, many of them keeping it "on the tab" for a long time. Sometimes it gets so long that Pa transfers it over to bills uncollectible. He asks them politely if they could just pay a little now and then. But most of them tell him different things, and he always nods his head in understanding.

"Wheat prices are down," some say. "We don't even break even these days."

"Lost my best gurnsey last week of fodder poisoning — and I still got vet bills to pay."

"The bottom 80 flooded during those rains last month. Got to plant the whole crop over."

"Kids got the croup and the missus is feeling poorly. Doctor bills are stacking up. Don't know when I'll be able to pay even a little. Much obliged to you for carrying me. You'll get your money; don't worry about that. It just takes time, that's all."

Pa always grinned painful-like and let the matter ride for the time being.

Pa, Ma, and me live in this little town named Belford, Kansas after the founder Johannes P. Belford who settled here in 1874. He got off the boat from Sweden a few months before and he and his young wife headed west to find a farm and to freely practice their Lutheran religion. They traveled by covered wagon, parting with the rest of the wagon train on their way to Oregon when they came upon this hazy blue valley nestled at the foot of the Flint Hills. I heard that Johannes Belford knew at first glance that this was where he wanted to live until he died. The valley was as green as could be and a muddy old river snaked through it, rimmed with rich sandy loam ready to produce any kind of farm product, from golden wheat to the reddest watermelons known to man.

I'm sure glad Johannes Belford found this little valley. His discovery gave me a chance to live here. The town never got more than three hundred fifty souls counting every cat and dog alive. It's a lot like being in the country without living in the country. It's an ideal place for boys to grow up. There's Turtle Creek nearby with fat wiggly bullheads. And there's Cave Springs, Hidden Valley and the beautiful Flint Hills to roam around in, letting you pretend everything from being a great explorer to a swashbuckling pirate.

Kids play in the streets way past dark in Belford. We just don't like to hang around the house much. There's too many exciting things to do. Even when winter comes and the snow drifts six feet high, kids pull on caps with wool flaps, big mackinaws, and seven buckle overshoes and play as though there's no snow at all.

Our house is smack dab next to the school yard. You just have to step off our yard and there you are on the school yard. This makes it handy. I can get up five minutes before the bell rings and have no trouble at all getting there on time. But I sort of like school, and I generally wait on the concrete steps for Mr. Sherberg to open up so we can play basketball in the gym before class. Even in the summer, when school is closed, I'm there with my friends. We get up on the roof of the gym and move a couple of metal bars away from the windows, then drop onto the bleachers and play ball for hours on end. The gang never disturbs anything. We just love to play basketball. We have dribbling contests, free throw contests, play H-O-R-S-E and Around-the-World — games like that.

Time seems to ooze by in Belford. We know we're never going to get old. Who thinks about getting old at twelve or thirteen? That's way off. Of course, we don't ask ourselves how Old Man Hughes got to be as old as he is. We don't dream that there was once a time when he was a kid around 12 or 13. I guess we think he was born with tons of wrinkles, inch-thick glasses and bunions. I don't know. We really never think about it much.

After nine months of school, I was looking forward to twelve slow- moving lazy weeks of freedom. I had a whole lot of things planned to do.

The sun was as hot as our potbellied stove after it's been stoked good on a winter's night. I hippity-hopped across the street for fear my bare feet might stick to the road. I had a dollar and some coins in my sweaty hand to buy some material for Ma at the store.

I looked up the hill. Belford was built on a hill; they never had to fear about flooding that way. I saw what looked like little wet, wavy patches floating in midair. Already, I was hot and thirsty and I hadn't even gone six blocks. My mouth was set on slurping a Green River at Peterson's Drugs. Ma said that if there was anything left out of the money after buying four yards of material I could get myself a Green River at Peterson's. I figured there should be at least a nickel left if I was lucky. You could buy a pretty nice Green River with a nickel. I hipped and hopped a little faster, just thinking about a nice cold drink and the ceiling fan going round over my head. It always seemed cooler there than anywhere else in town. And I really liked the smell of everything mixed together. I could smell the ladies' powder and cosmetics, the lemons and limes behind the fountain, and even the new ink on the papers and magazines in the news rack. I loved to leaf through the comics and maybe even buy one. Once the cashier decided to tape them shut because so many kids came in and bought a nickel Green River or a nickel Coca Cola and spent the whole afternoon reading Captain Marvel, Dick Tracy, Wonderwoman, Superman, and some of the others without buying a single copy. Some of them peeled the tape back. I caught a lot of them doing that. The Petersons finally decided to forget the tape.

Today, Ma made me wear my shirt. I felt the cotton cloth cling to my back as sweat poured off me. She thought it wasn't proper not to wear a shirt to town. I knew I'd peel it right back off when I got home again. She never made me wear shoes, though. No kid wore shoes in the summer except to church or fancy affairs like ice cream socials, band concerts, or political rallies.

I mopped my brow with my fist wadded with money and looked up ahead. My heart sank to the bottom of my feet. There was Mick Fuller and his gang coming toward me. I squinted my eyes in the sun to be sure who was with him. I knew the tall one was Mick because he carried a staff. Actually, it was just a pole he cut the branches off of. But he always carried it. I think he thought it made him look important or something. Frank was with him. You couldn't miss Frank because he was about as wide as he was tall. The fat kind of laid over his eyes. Some kids used to laugh and say it was easier to jump over him than walk around him. His face was sweaty and red as a beet. He was trailing Mick as usual, partly because he was so fat he couldn't keep up and partly because Mick didn't like

4

anyone walking in front of him or beside him. He was the leader and he wanted everyone to remember it. Walking back with Frank was Lowell. Lowell was an albino. His hair was snow white and his eyes were pale blue rimmed with pink skin. His eyebrows and eyelashes were so white it looked as though he didn't have any. Clancy and Donder weren't with Mick today. It was just the three of them plus Mick's red chow-chow, Devil. That was the meanest looking and meanest acting dog in town. He was bright red and had a mane like a lion. There were a lot of dogs in town carrying scars or limping because of Devil. Mick was proud as a peacock over his dog. He knew he could fight like the dickens and win every fight he got into.

"Where you going, Bimberg? Going on an errand for mommy?" Mick asked, grinning as he approached.

"Yeah, so what?" I said, hunching my shoulders.

Mick stood straddle-legged in my way with Frank and Lowell on either side. I would've had to walk on Mrs. Salsburg's marigolds or go into the street to get by them.

"How about treating me and the boys to a Green River at Peterson's, or better yet, some hard cider at the pool hall?" he asked.

I knew he was just trying to act tough. "I don't have any extra money," I replied. "I've got just enough for my Ma's material and that's all." I sort of lied because I was still planning on having enough for a drink of my own.

"That ain't very neighborly of you, Bimberg," Mick said, nudging his straw hat back from his forehead.

I looked into Mick's face blotched with about a million freckles. In fact, in some places they just poured together in big brown patches. His bright red hair was pasted with sweat to his forehead.

"I can't help it, Mick," I said. "I haven't got any extra money for anything. Just enough for what Ma sent me for."

"And I still say that ain't neighborly of you one bit. Right, boys?" Frank and Lowell obediently nodded their heads.

5

I knew that Mick had heard that expression from the free picture show on Saturday nights between the burned out walls of Seiwalds and the Citizen's Bank. John Wayne used it a whole lot.

"Maybe I should sic Devil on you? Maybe that would make you act a little more neighborly."

I shook my head, starting around him. Devil growled and his upper lip drew back exposing a row of sharp white fangs. I acted as though Devil didn't bother me one bit, but I felt my heart pound in my chest as I dipped down into the gutter and back up on the sidewalk.

Mick turned around, his face red as fire. "Bimberg, you just about got your tail bit. You know that?"

I walked on, acting as though I hadn't heard a thing Mick said. With my eyes on the ground, I silently counted the bricks in front of my feet.

"Hey, Bimberg! Did you hear what I said?"

I turned around, looking back over my shoulder. "Yeah, I heard you. So what?"

Mick and his boys ran up behind me. My stomach tightened, getting ready for battle. You never knew what Mick had in mind. I tensed, feeling his hand touch my shoulder.

"Hey, Bimberg...don't go away mad. I just want to talk to you, that's all."

I kept right on walking. I felt the damp dollar and the wet coins clumped together in my fist.

"Hold up, will you?" he yelled.

I stopped and turned to face him.

"We just thought you might have changed your mind. You've had plenty of time to think about it."

"I told you that I've got just enough for my Ma's material and that's all. I ain't about to..."

"Naaww..." Mick said, grinning. "That ain't what I wanted to talk about. Right, boys?"

Frank and Lowell shook their heads.

"It's about the club. You decided to come on in with us

or not? You've had a long time to think about it. It's the best club in town." He offered me his plug of tobacco. "Here, take a chaw. That should show you I'm trying to be friends. It's Red Man and it's as strong as anything you can buy. That is, if you're man enough to take a chaw..." He leaned forward, grinning, letting a liquid line of black spit ooze from his mouth.

Frank and Lowell looked at each other and laughed.

"Give me that thing," I said. I wasn't about to let Mick Fuller think I couldn't handle tobacco even though I got as sick as a dog last year experimenting with Troop behind his folks' shed. I bit into the plug, working the tobacco up and down in my mouth. For a moment my eyes went back in my head and a wave of dizziness swept over me. I jumped to one side, blaming the hot sidewalk for burning my feet.

"What's the matter...too strong?" Mick said, expertly spitting the juice on the sidewalk before him.

"Naw, it ain't that. These bricks are burning my feet, that's all."

"Oh, that's it, huh?" Mick said over his shoulder at Frank and Lowell. "Glad you're such an expert at chewing. I was afraid you might get sick or something."

"Naw. Never did bother me. In fact, I like it. I have it quite a bit at home after supper or during chores. Times like that."

"Sure, I'll just bet," Mick said with a sneer.

I stood there facing him, eyeball to eyeball. Meanwhile the tobacco juice drained down my throat feeling more like cactus juice.

"Let's go," whined Frank. "He ain't going to treat us to no Green River or Coke. If he's going to be that way, let him."

"Bimberg's always been against us," Mick said, as he ran his hand through Devil's mane. "We've invited him to join the club many times and he's always turned his nose up at it. Thinks he's too good, I guess."

I swallowed some of the tobacco juice, feeling tears well up in my eyes. "It ain't that, Mick. Some of us guys have a club already. You know that. We've never felt like joining any other, that's all."

"Sure. You think you're too good for us." Mick looked over his shoulder again. "Ain't that right, fellas?"

Frank and Lowell said "yes", and Devil growled, baring his teeth.

"We've got some of the best stuff you ever saw in our club, Bimberg. Our initiation ain't for cry babies, that's for sure. You've got to be a real man to pass all the tests." He paused and cocked his head to one side. "Your club have an initiation?"

"Sure," I said. "We've got a real tough one."

"What do you make them do?" Frank called out. "See who can knit faster than the others, or what?"

Lowell giggled, tossing his white hair back. "Or maybe they make them eat a bunch of those dainty little sandwiches," he said.

I felt my face getting red again. This time it wasn't the tobacco. I was hot mad. "Well, you guys will never know, will you? That's our club and our secret initiation and everything is our business. And since you're not members you'll never know our business."

Mick threw down his staff, rushed forward, and grabbed me by the collar. I heard that sickening sound of cloth tearing and knew Ma would be upset when I got home. Devil came up growling right by my leg. I felt his drool and his hot breath.

"You listen to me, smart guy. Nobody talks to Mick Fuller like that. Everybody in town knows I'm tougher than anyone else. You get smart and you'll find your teeth laying on the ground."

I felt a rush of fear race to the top of my head. Although Mick was a lot of hot air most of the time, he would do just what he said some of the time. And when he got into a fight, anything went. He thought nothing of gouging a guy's eyes or biting ears, kicking shins or elbowing stomachs. I jammed the coins and the bill down in my pocket and pushed his arm back to pretend I wasn't scared. "Let me alone, Mick. This all started when I said I didn't have enough money to buy you guys a drink. Now, I still say I don't have enough money. No matter if you all gang up on me and beat me up, I still won't have enough money. But, if you want to take me on one-on-one, I'll fight you right here and I'll prove it." I took a boxer's stance.

Mick looked down at me, his little beady eyes blazing. He was testing me, and he knew I knew it. Finally, he jerked his hand loose and stepped back, laughing.

"Come on, guys. Bimberg ain't worth fooling with. If he wants to take his money and do what his mommy wants, that's his problem. He won't ever get a chance to see our cow skull or see our mascot."

"Yeah," Frank and Lowell cried out together.

Mick's eyes squinted real tight. "But, you can be sure that it's war between your club and ours and the Spiders will be on top every time."

"What do you call your club, Bimberg?" Frank asked, hiking up a strap on his bib overalls.

"Probably the ladies afternoon tea party," Lowell said with a snicker.

Mick laughed, showing his tobacco stained teeth. He turned and spit, nearly hitting Devil in the head. The dog reared back and eyed Mick a bit strangely.

"It's the 'Mustangs' if it's any of your business," I said defensively.

Each one looked at the others. I could tell they were trying to think of something funny to say about the name 'Mustangs', but they couldn't come up with anything.

Mick jerked his head to one side as he thought of something. "Well, I tell you what. I, being the president of the Spiders, challenge your club to meet us out at Cave

Springs to settle all of this." He paused and rolled his eyes back in his head in thought. "Let's make it tonight at midnight at the foot of Cave Springs Mountain. We'll see who has the best club then. We'll settle all of this."

I knew that you had to watch Mick real careful. You never knew what he had up his sleeve. It could be a trap. I sure wished Troop was here to help me decide. Him being my best friend and all. Of course, I also knew that if I backed down it would look like me and the rest of the Mustangs were chicken. I had to do it for the club's honor. Another problem was getting out at that time of night. I knew that Mick could get out any time he wanted. His folks couldn't care less. His Pa was usually up at the pool hall and his Ma was too busy taking care of all of Mick's brothers and sisters. He always roamed around town late at night with his staff and Devil following at his side. His folks just didn't care. I guess I felt a little sorry for him, even though Mick claimed he was the luckiest kid in town, beings he always got to do what he wanted without some parent giving him orders and all.

"Well, what do you say, Bimberg? The cat got your tongue or are you just chicken?" Mick asked in a little sing-song voice.

"Me and the boys will be there. Tonight at the bottom of Cave Springs Mountain at midnight." I nodded sharply. "Okay, you got yourself a deal."

Mick looked skeptically at his pals and then back at me. "How you going to get away that late without your old man knowing it?"

I jabbed a thumb in my chest. "Let me worry about that. You just show up there tonight, that's all."

"I ain't worrying about it, Bimberg. I ain't worrying at all," Mick said.

"I'll be there with Troop for sure."

Mick studied his pals for a few moments and then looked down at Devil, debating whether there was anything else left to say. Finally, he shrugged and nodded for Frank and Lowell to follow him down the street. "Let's go. We'll see if Mr. Big Shot will show up there or if he chickens out. We'll just see," he sneered.

"Yeah, we'll see," said Frank.

Lowell looked at me with his pale blue eyes rimmed in pink skin and shrugged. He didn't say anything.

Mick jerked the brim of his hat back down over his eyes and nudged Devil with his staff. Devil jumped and obeyed at once. The three of them went on down the sidewalk, throwing rocks at cats and spitting tobacco juice all over the sidewalk.

Chapter 2

"How many eggs did you get today?"

"Only fifteen," I said, setting the bucket down on a chair.

Ma shook her head. "That isn't very good. Fifteen out of thirty-two pullets. I suppose it's the heat." She was looking down at the mound of dough setting before her.

"Yeah, I suppose," I said as I scooted my bare feet along the linoleum until I got to the ice box.

"Don't leave the door open too long today. That's a new cake of ice and I want it to last awhile."

"Okay." I pulled out a bottle of milk and poured myself a glassful. I tipped the glass and drained half of it. It wasn't very cold but it tasted real good on such a scorcher of a day.

"Empty the drain pan when you're through," Ma said while adding more flour to the clump of dough.

"Okay. Any cookies around?"

Ma looked around, pretending to be stern. "My stars. I never saw a boy who could eat like you. Don't you have any bottom to that stomach?"

"Pa says I'm growing. When you're growing you've got to eat to fill out those bones that's stretching up and out."

"Yes, and someday you'll stop and then it'll all go to your stomach or other places."

"Someday's a long way off, Ma. I'm hungry right now."

"There's a plate of fresh-baked oatmeal and raisin cookies in the cupboard. Be sure and put the rag back over them to keep the flies away. They're bad today." She rubbed the back of her neck. "It must be the humidity or something. Probably a storm coming up."

I pulled a chair over to the cupboard and climbed on it, knowing right where Ma always puts the fresh-baked cookies. I could smell them before I lifted the cloth. They were big and generous and chewy. I liked them better than any of the other kids' mas' cookies in town. Some of them skimped on the raisins and oatmeal. Not Ma's cookies; they were man-sized.

I took two and put the cloth back over the rest. I settled back down with a glass in one hand and a cookie in the other.

Ma placed the dough in bread pans and set them near the window to rise. She finished by placing a damp cloth over them. "We'll have bread tonight for supper."

I never knew why she said that because we always had fresh-baked bread. But she always said that when she finished. I leaned back in my chair with the two front legs rearing up. I settled them back down when I saw her warning glance.

"What would you do...," I started.

"Wait 'til you finish swallowing before you talk. Never talk with your mouth full. How many times have I told you?"

I swallowed. "What would you do if someone put a big dare on you?"

She brushed the flour from her hands. "Depends who put the dare on me and what the dare was, I suppose."

"I know. But, suppose it was someone you didn't like all that much. You felt like you kind of had to take him up on the dare because it's like a test."

Ma placed her hands on her hips and blew back a wisp of hair that had fallen over her forehead. "What are you getting at, Carlisle?"

I made a face. I hated my full name. Everybody called me Carley. I was named after my ma's side of the family, the Carlisles. "Ma, you promised you'd never call me that," I said.

"I didn't promise you anything like that. I said I'd try to remember not to call you that in public. You said it embarrassed you." She looked around. "Is this out in public? If it is, I don't see any people." She smiled.

14

I knew she was teasing me and I laughed. "You know what I mean. That name sounds funny. I like Carley a lot better."

"All right, Carley. Now, what is this all about?" she asked.

"I just wanted to know if a person felt that he had to do something, should he do it even though this something might get him into a peck of trouble." I thought for a moment. "But, not doing it might get him into trouble."

Ma shook her head soberly. "Carley, I don't know. In fact, I don't really know what you're talking about."

"I just wondered if someone told you you had better do something because if you didn't it would prove something to him worse than if you didn't do something...would you do it?"

Ma's eyebrows raised clear up near her hair. "Why don't you go wash those eggs and put them in the cartons. Put them on down in the cellar. We'll have enough to take to the creamery in two or three more days."

"But, you didn't answer me," I cried.

Ma placed her hands on her hips. "How can I answer you when I don't even know what you're talking about?"

I scratched my head. "Gee, I thought I explained it pretty good."

Ma pointed her finger toward the bucket of eggs. "March!" she ordered.

I knew that there was no use trying to talk to her. When Ma said 'march', a fella might as well give in. There was no way I was going to get an answer. Still, I thought I explained it as plain as day.

I carried the bucket out to the faucet in the back yard. Squatting down, I turned on the water. Before you know it, I had three eggs clean as could be.

I was busy with the eggs and thinking about what I was going to do when I felt a finger poke my shoulder.

"What're you doing, Carley?"

I knew right away it was Troop. Only Troop crept up real quiet-like to surprise you. He was a full-blooded Cherokee. Actually, Troop's name is Bryan Whitewater. His pa and ma live in Belford now, but they used to live on a reservation in South Dakota. Five years ago they moved here so his pa could help lay ties for the railroad. Neither his ma or pa could speak any English, but Troop can talk as good as me. Troop's been my best friend for years and years. I never saw a guy who could walk so quiet. Not even a blade of grass moves...not even a twig snaps. One time I was out fishing and after about an hour I happened to look up and there he was in a tree crotch watching everything I was doing. He said he'd been there for about an hour. I never did know how he got up there without me seeing him. He was all Cherokee, all right.

"What does it look like I'm doing?" I replied. "I sure ain't playing baseball or kick-the-can. I sure ain't fishing for crawdads. And I sure ain't quail hunting." I was kind of proud the way I could talk.

Troop looked confused. "You're washing eggs. Anybody can see that."

"Well, that's what I'm doing, washing eggs." I scrubbed a hard piece of gunk off a shell.

Troop sat down beside me, crossing his legs.

I looked up. A bunch of black hair was over one of his eyes. He wore a beat up straw hat and torn overalls. He never wore a shirt or shoes except when it was real cold.

"I've got a real problem, Troop," I said quietly, looking carefully toward the back door.

"What is it?"

I sighed, scrubbing that one egg. I was about ready to wear out the shell. "Well, I saw Mick, Frank, and Lowell when I went up town today. Devil was with them looking like a big red lion with that mane and all. He just about bit me on the tail."

"What was it all about? Why did you run into them?"

"Well, Ma sent me up town to get her some material. Here they came down the hill as big as you please. Mick had his staff and Frank and Lowell were following him as usual. Devil was tagging at his side. At first they blocked my way. I finally got around them and Mick came up grabbing me by the shoulder and Devil started growling."

"Did you guys fight?" Troop asked, jerking at the brim of his hat excitedly.

"Naw. For a few moments I thought we might, but it didn't turn into one. He asked me again to join the Spiders. I told him we already had a club. One thing led to another and finally he backed me up into a corner with a dare." I swallowed hard. "I said I'd meet him out at Cave Springs tonight at midnight."

"You going?" Troop asked.

"I've got to. He'll think I'm chicken if I don't." I shrugged and picked up another egg. "Of course Mick can come and go as he pleases. His folks don't care. Ma would skin me alive if she caught me out at that time of night."

"What are you going to do?" Troop asked.

I looked around at him. "I've got to go, that's all. You should know that. When a guy like Mick gives you a dare, you've got to take it."

"You'd better watch yourself, Carley. Mick can be real mean. It's hard to tell what he wants clear out there at Cave Springs."

I nodded. "I know. But right now I'm more worried about being able to get out of the house tonight. My folks are light sleepers and they keep the house locked tighter than a drum."

Troop got to his feet and walked around to the south side of the house. He looked up at my second story bedroom window. "No problem," he shouted.

"Shhh! Don't talk so loud. I don't want Ma to hear you."

Troop pointed at the window. He lowered his voice. "All

you have to do is jump from your bedroom window and grab that limb there on that elm tree."

"What? You must be crazy! That limb is six to eight feet from the window. I could kill myself."

Troop shook his head disappointedly. "Ah, come on, Carley. It's not that far away. Just boost yourself and jump. You grab the limb and then shinny down the tree. It's simple."

"Yeah, but I'm not you. I can't climb like a monkey." I studied the situation for several moments. At last my face lit up. I had thought of a great solution.

"What?" Troop asked.

"Well, what about this? I get a slat from my bed and prop it against my window sill and on the limb. Then all I've got to do is crawl along the slat and climb down the tree. Also, the slat is still there when I want to get back into my room. I climb up the tree, walk along the slat, pull it in when I'm across, and put it back beneath my bed. No one's the wiser." I brushed my hands together in a final gesture.

Troop thought about it for a moment. He nodded, smiling. "I think you've got a good idea, Carley. That just might work."

"Now, how about you?" I asked. "Are you going to be able to get out that late and meet me to go to Cave Springs? You're the vice-president of the Mustangs, you know."

"Sure," he said. "It's easy. I crawl out of my window all the time. Of course, I sleep on the first floor."

I laughed, batting him hard with my ball cap.

Ma looked out the back door to see what all the ruckus was. She looked at me and she looked at the bucket of eggs still setting beside the faucet to get clean. I took the hint and walked back over to finish my chore.

Troop grabbed an egg and started cleaning it with a wet rag. "What do you think Mick's got on his mind out there that late?"

"I don't know. But like you said, with Mick you never know. He's always thinking up something."

The both of us sat in silence for a long time until we finished cleaning the eggs. Finally they were stacked carefully back in the bucket ready to go to the cellar.

Troop got to his feet and stretched. He looked down at me, still working on the last egg. "I'll meet you out at the curve just before you get to Hagan's barn. I'll be sitting in the culvert. When I see you coming, I'll give out our secret whistle."

I nodded. "Sounds good." I loved that secret whistle. It was three longs and a short in sort of a trill like the sound of a meadowlark. Just the Mustangs knew about it.

"Should we tell any of the others to meet us?" I asked.

"No. Most of them would be too afraid of getting in trouble with their parents at that time of night. Just you and I should go as president and vice-president of the Mustangs."

"Right. I think that's best." I got to my feet and picked up the bucket. "Well, I'll see you out at the curve just before Hagan's barn then. Be there about fifteen minutes before midnight. It takes another fifteen or twenty minutes to get to Cave Springs Mountain."

"Right," Troop said, turning to leave. "See you then."

"Right," I replied.

Ma stuck her head out the back door once more. She had a frown on her face. I held up the bucket of eggs. "All done, Ma. I'm on my way to the cellar right now."

Everything had been quiet downstairs for a long time. I was sure Ma and Pa were fast asleep. I heard the radio go off and heard Pa's shoes drop to the floor over an hour ago. Once, I opened my bedroom door and it was dark as pitch so I knew there were no lights downstairs. Carefully, I lifted my pillow and shined a flashlight on my pocketwatch. It was one of my prized possessions. Pa gave it to me for my birthday last year. I had looked at it in Franklin's Jewelry store for weeks. I couldn't believe it when I opened the package on my birthday and there it was in a bunch of cotton. It was the prettiest thing I ever saw engraved with heads of wheat in 14 karat gold. I know it must've cost a fortune.

Eleven fifteen. I thought about the time it would take to get the slat out from under my mattress, put it in the elm tree, and get down and then run out to meet Troop. I nodded to myself. Yeah, it was time to get going.

I got out of bed and slipped on my pants and shirt. The floor creaked beneath my feet. Carefully I lifted the bottom of my mattress and eased out a wooden slat. I bumped it into everything in the dark. But I didn't want to chance turning on my light. I imagined that any moment I'd hear the sound of Pa's bare feet coming up the stairs to see what I was up to. Finally, I got the slat out and tugged on the window to open it. It took all my strength because of the old paint and the humidity swelling the wood. At last, it slid open and I pushed the slat through it.

The moon was full and bright as a new silver dollar. I saw the limb hanging there in the night perfectly. I pushed the slat to the crook of the limb so it wouldn't slide one way or the other once I got on it. I stuck my flashlight in my back pocket, pushed my pocketwatch in my front pocket, and took a deep breath. My heart beat like a drum as I leaned forward and climbed onto the slat. It wobbled one way and then the other when I got on all fours to cross it.

The night air smelled of honeysuckle from the bushes near our front porch. I heard dogs barking about a block down the street. Every light in the neighborhood was out. I felt as if I was the only kid on earth up and going. It was a real funny feeling. I started across the slat. Once, I looked down and gulped. It was a ways down if I fell or if

20

the board broke. I knew a fella could break his leg or arm from that distance. Maybe even his neck. Instead of looking down any more, I looked straight ahead. Halfway there, I stopped to get my breath. The wind was blowing a little up there and it felt good because I was sweating bad. The slat bowed down in the middle and I scampered forward, afraid it was going to crack at any minute. Once I stepped on the solid limb I pushed the end of the board deeper into the crook of the tree. The slat was in tight. I didn't want a wind to come up or anything and cause it to fall while I was away. I would be in deep trouble then because the house was locked solid. Getting down the tree was no trouble. There were strong limbs to hold my weight. Before I knew it, I was on the ground racing across the schoolyard and across Boswell's vacant lot and garden and then beyond the city limits.

Chapter 3

I didn't have any trouble getting out of town. I didn't even meet one car or see one sign of life. Markley's dog, Chipper, came out of his yard barking but when he saw it was me, he stood there watching me his tail wagging as fast as could be. He knew me because I delivered their newspaper.

Gravel dug at my feet. I aimed the flashlight down ahead of me so I wouldn't hurt my feet any worse than I had to. Sometimes I'd walk in a muddy tire track. That was a whole lot easier.

About a mile out of town I stopped and fished out my pocketwatch. Twenty minutes 'til twelve. I was making good time. I'd be close to the curve where Troop said he'd be in about five more minutes. I was timing everything just right. I felt pretty proud of myself.

As I ran down the road, I saw heavy black shadows of stone fences bordering the pastures. I knew how long and how hard it was to build those fences. I also knew that they would last hundreds of years. Now and then I heard the creak of a windmill spinning in the night. Big dark mounds lay out in the fields. They were cattle resting with the full moon casting its light down on them.

It came faintly from the distance. Three longs and a short: a trill like a meadowlark. I flashed my light into the dark and whistled back. Sure enough, there was Troop sitting in a ditch as big as you please about twenty yards away. He waved his hat and whistled again. I waved my cap, returning the whistle. I felt better knowing that he showed up even though I really wasn't that much afraid he wouldn't.

"Have any trouble getting out, Carley?" Troop asked.

I shook my head. "Naw...easy as pie."

Troop ran like a deer, but I wasn't too bad either. We

kept even pace for the entire half mile. After about five minutes Troop nodded sharply, and we went to the left, fighting
our way through thick grass and weeds taller than our
heads. Sharp sticks and rocks poked my feet. Once I stubbed
my toe on a rock buried in the dirt. I just about cussed out
loud but I held it in by biting my tongue. My eyes watered
as my toe throbbed. Big stalks whapped me in the face, and
seeds and milk pods got down my neck and started itching.
It was downright miserable fighting our way through those
weeds. After about ten minutes we got through it and
walked out on a shelf of smooth rock. The rushing springs
running over the rocks sounded in the distance.

"See anything of Mick and his gang?" I asked Troop.

Troop shook his head.

We walked toward the springs. I had never been out
there before at night. It sure looked different. Things
familiar just weren't there. Everything looked kind of
spooky. The branches hung down like fingers coming out
of the sky. A big barn owl swooped out of a tree over our
heads. Troop and I lunged back, crashing into each
other. We both felt the breeze of its wings.

"Criminy!" I screamed. "That was close!"

"There's Mick," Troop said, pointing straight ahead.

I strained my eyes but I couldn't see anything.
"Where?"

"Over there. He's got two guys with him and he's got
Devil."

Troop could see like a cat in the dark. I took his word
for it and followed him toward Mick and the gang.

"So you did show up after all, Bimberg?" Mick said
snotty-like.

Finally, I saw him. He was sitting on a boulder running
his fingers through Devil's thick mane.

"I told you I would," I said, sounding just as snotty.

"Brought the Indian with you, I see."

"Yeah, so what?" I said.

"Yeah, so what?" Troop said.

When I got closer I saw Frank squatting down on a rock beside Lowell. Lowell really showed up in the dark with his white hair and white skin. He sort of glowed in the dark.

Devil turned his head toward us and growled. I saw his white teeth flash in the dark.

"What's this all about, Mick? Me and Troop are both here like I said we'd be. Now it's your move. What's the big mystery?"

"I thought you two would have trouble getting away from your mas but you fooled me all right." He looked over at Frank and Lowell and they giggled.

"Quit stalling, Mick," I said. "Tell us what you have planned. Make it quick or we're going to turn around and go back and climb into bed."

Mick waved his hand. "Okay, hold your horses. Don't get mad."

I couldn't see his eyes beneath his hat but I knew they were all squinty.

Picking up his flashlight, he beamed it above him. "That."

"What, that?" I asked. "What are you talking about?"

"What I want has nothing to do with the Indian. It has to do with you, Bimberg. This is part of the Spider's initiation...climbing Cave Springs Mountain."

"What?" I asked.

"You become deaf or what all of a sudden? I'm saying that I'll match you to a climb. Cave Springs Mountain has been climbed a few times in the daytime but never at night. I'm challenging you to a climb at night, Bimberg."

Squiggly things started crawling around in my belly and my mouth got as dry as cotton. I beamed my light up the side of Cave Springs Mountain. Of course, it wasn't really a mountain. It was a hill...but what a hill! It went straight up. There was nothing but shale and loose rock on the sides. Every step you took felt like you were walking on egg shells. Your feet would find a hold and then suddenly there'd be nothing there but air and the rocks and shale would roll to the bottom. There had been one kid who got killed on it when my Pa was a boy. He lost his footing, fell clear to the bottom and hit his head on a boulder. Once you got to the top you took another way down. That was no problem, but going up was real scary.

"Nobody climbs Cave Springs Mountain at night. You'd have to be a fool to do that. You're just asking to get killed," I said hopefully.

"I thought so," Mick said, glancing down at Frank and Lowell. "I told you it'd be too much for Bimberg. He's chicken." He wrinkled his nose and shook his head. "We wouldn't want anybody like him in our club anyway."

"I'll climb it," Troop said, walking toward Mick.

"Not on your life. You're an Indian. You're a natural climber. I want Bimberg here, to do it. He's your president, and I'm the president of the Spiders, so that's who has to go up."

I couldn't see his mouth but I knew he was grinning. I knew Frank and Lowell were grinning too, even though I couldn't see them. I swallowed hard. "I guess he's right," I said weakly.

"You're not going to climb Cave Springs Mountain at night are you, Carley? Don't be crazy. Remember, a kid fell and got himself killed years ago," Troop said, grabbing my shirt.

I talked real soft. "I've got to. Don't you understand that? It's me Mick gave the dare to. He's the president of the Spiders and I'm president of the Mustangs. It's got to be me."

"Why don't you let me go up for you? You said yourself I'm a better climber than you," Troop argued.

It kind of plugged up my throat when Troop said that. In other words, he was willing to risk his life for me. I knew we'd be buddies forever. I shook my head. "Nope. It's got to be me and that's that. If I take it real slow and careful-like it shouldn't be any problem."

"Hey, what's all the jawing?" Mick shouted. "You going

up or not, Bimberg? Maybe you're chicken. Make up your mind. Me and the boys are getting tired of waiting."

I heard a growly rumble come out of the darkness from Devil.

I fished my watch out of my pocket and handed it to Troop. "Here. You hold on to this. I don't want to break it. My Pa gave it to me on my last birthday. It's got wheat engraved on it and says 'To Carley from Pa'. It means a whole lot to me. Besides, it's 14 karat gold plated."

Troop took it and put it in his pocket. He patted my shoulder as if to say he'd take care of it because I wasn't about to come back. I handed him the flashlight, too, because I knew I'd need both hands free to hold on to everything I could going up.

"You ready, Bimberg?" Mick asked, shining his flashlight in my eyes.

My mouth was almost too dry to speak. My voice started to come out in a squeak, but I lowered it immediately. "Yeah, I'm ready."

"Okay, let's go."

Mick and I walked across the spring to the base of the hill. Little jagged edges of shale gouged the soles of my feet. I didn't say anything because Mick was barefoot too, and he never let on that it bothered him at all.

Mick stopped and looked straight up. "Now, we both start out here and climb straight up. The one who reaches the top first is the winner and his club is the best." He flashed his light along the slick wall of the hill.

I shivered. Quickly, while the light was there, I searched out roots and rocks for toe and hand holds. And then it was dark again.

"Want a chaw before we start to climb, Bimberg?"

He offered me his plug. "Naw...I'll have one when I get down and celebrate as the winner."

"Sure, Bimberg, sure." He bit into the plug and worked the tobacco around his mouth, finally storing it in a wet pocket of his cheek. He threw his flashlight to Frank and turned. "You ready, Bimberg?"

"Yeah," I said. "Let's go!"

"Go!" shouted Mick, scrambling forward. I felt like a snail next to him. Mick was already six feet up the side of the hill when I got started. I heard Troop and Mick's gang shouting across the spring. I sort of jumped on the side of the hill like I was getting on a horse or something. Looking up, I saw Mick's bare feet flying above me.

Luckily, my feet hit on cool, solid rock and I climbed five steps just as easy as going up my bedroom stairs. This ain't no step for a stepper. Suddenly, I felt bigger than life. Confidence poured through me.

"Keep going, Carley. You're doing great!" Troop yelled from below.

I was glad Troop was there. He always stood beside me no matter what. I looked straight up. Even though the moon was bright and full, it was still as dark as a gravedigger's closet, as my grandpa always said. Suddenly, I got a mouthful of dust and pebbles. I stopped to spit and cough. It felt as if I had mud balls in my mouth.

"Did you get a snoot full?" Mick shouted from above.

I decided not to answer.

My feet were still getting some good holds. But I discovered I couldn't stay in one place over a second or the rock would give way like rotten egg shells.

Looking up, I saw Mick scrambling upward. He grunted and something heavy, probably his chest, hit the side of the hill. It sounded as if his wind had been knocked clear out of him. Dust and rocks rolled past and then came his straw hat following right behind. I heard him cuss.

Looking up, I saw him clinging to a root, panting like a fat dog, trying to catch his breath.

"Everything all right up there?" Troop yelled from below.

I swallowed and glanced down. Right away I knew I shouldn't have done that. I was a whole lot higher than I thought I was. Troop looked like a toy down there. I saw the black clumps of boulders around the bottom. In the silent summer night the rush of the springs came to my ears. "Sure, Troop, everything's fine," I called.

I gulped and started on up. I took one careful step at a time. Then my feet slipped and I started falling. My hands and feet flew in every direction trying to catch hold. My heart leaped into my throat. In my mind I saw my brains squashed all over a boulder down there. I dug my fingers into the sides of the hill until they ached, while my feet dangled in mid-air.

"Oh, Lord, help me now. Please help me now," I murmured. Sweat poured down my face. My shirt stuck like glue to my back.

The Lord must've heard me because about that time my hand hit a tough old root sticking out the side of the hill and I clung to it like it was gold. My feet waved in the air, searching for a hold. I dug my toes into the loose shale and just stayed there, too scared to holler.

I stayed there for about two minutes, wondering what I should do. It was straight down and it was straight up. I didn't think the Lord was going to work two miracles tonight after saving me once. I was about in the middle so I decided to go ahead and try it on up. It sure wasn't doing me any good dangling there like Ma's wash on the line. With all my might I gave a grunt and pulled myself up, holding the root with one hand while my other hand felt the side of the hill for another hold. Digging my toes in like cat claws, I made it up another three or four feet.

I looked up at Mick. He looked down, his teeth flashing in the dark.

"I don't know, Bimberg. What if I slipped and some rocks fell and hit you on the head? You'd probably let go and fall clear down to the bottom, wouldn't you?" He pushed a few pieces of shale and rock down on me.

I gritted my teeth, feeling my face go blood red I was so

mad. "Either climb on up or get out of my way, Mick. I want to get home sometime tonight and get back to bed." I tried to sound brave.

"Sure, sure. Hold your horses. I'm still going to beat you by a mile. That's a sure fact. I'm better than you, and the Spiders are better than the Mustangs."

Dirt and small rocks coated me again about that time. "Oops," Mick said with a laugh. I couldn't swear but I'm almost sure Mick planned that little accidental rock slide.

I got madder and more determined than ever. Someday, I vowed right then, I was going to teach Mick Fuller a lesson. I struggled up another four steps. The guys below disappeared from my sight although I still heard their voices and the springs running over the rocks.

Mick continued climbing, his dust, dirt, and rocks landing on me below him. Sweat ran all over me. My back was sopping wet. Reaching up, I grabbed a rock and hauled myself up further. I slipped and slid down two yards until my foot hit a solid rock. I felt a little trickle of blood leak out of the palm of my hand.

"Hey, Bimberg," Mick shouted. "I can see the top. I'll be perched up there in about a couple of minutes. I told you we had tough initiations. I'll be king of the mountain just like I always am."

I couldn't argue that fact with him. He was only a little ways away from the top. He'd be sitting there as pretty as you please, watching me splitting a gut trying to get there. Once again, Mick Fuller would have his way.

I shook off my anger and started up once again, slipping and sliding two feet down and struggling up three or four feet. My hands and feet were raw. I was making some kind of headway. At least, Mick couldn't say that I didn't make it to the top.

"I'm just about there, Bimberg. Get ready to accept defeat. You ain't even close to being the man I am. You ain't...EEEEEOOOOO!!"

I heard what sounded like a screech owl caught by his pin feathers. And then rocks hit me on the face and shoulders. And then the whole hill shook and Mick streaked by as fast as greased lightning, hollering his lungs out. He was on his behind, falling like a rock, sliding as though he was on a giant slipper slide. He yelled clear to the bottom. Then I heard a giant splash. Devil barked his head off, and Frank and Lowell shouted.

I thought I heard then, but I'm not sure, Troop giving out a shrill war whoop, while Mick cussed in the background. Instead of just standing there, I crawled one agonizing step at a time to the top. I grabbed a clump of weeds and hoisted myself over the top. I laid on my back, sweating and panting like crazy.

After a couple of minutes, I got up and yelled clear to the bottom. "Troop! Troop! Can you hear me?"

I listened real careful.

"Carley, did you make it to the top?"

"Yeah!" I shouted. "I'm up here right now. It looks like I'm on the top of the whole world from up here. It looks like I can just reach up and touch the moon." I took a deep breath and let it out. "Hey, how's Mick? Did he make it to the bottom?"

"He made it all right," yelled Troop.

"Did he get hurt?"

"He landed in the spring. The only thing that's hurt is his pride and the seat of his pants. He tore them clean out!"

I know it ain't right to gloat when you win. Ma and Pa always told me to be a gracious winner. But I raised my hand and shouted in victory to that old moon!

Chapter 4

There was this one farmer. His name was Luke Webster. He was kind of crazy. Everyone knew it. He lived far out from Belford "out in the sticks". There was nobody who could raise better cattle or better crops than Luke Webster. But the crazy thing about it was that he sold just enough cattle to live on and he let the rest die of old age or allowed their horns to grow into their skulls. His wheat would be ripe and ready to harvest and he'd just let it go until it got a rust disease or set a torch to it, and then he'd replant again in the spring. Corn stalks, heavy with ears, just stayed in the field. People passed his property, which was always posted with skull-and-crossbones signs that said "No trespassing," and they wagged their heads at the sight of it all, knowing that that was the way Luke Webster was. No one dared step one foot on his property because he promised he'd shoot anyone who did. Luke was a quiet man. He lived clear out there with his older sister, Anna. Hardly anyone ever heard him say a word. He was big, with wide shoulders, and he grew a long beard clear to his belt. He always wore the same soiled, ten gallon hat pulled low over his forehead. His deep-set black eyes peered out from beneath it.

Luke had an old Ford pickup, but he preferred to ride his big, muscular buckskin gelding.

About once every two or three months, Luke came riding into town on that big horse. Everyone along the Belford streets crouched back, eyeing him suspiciously. Little kids ran to their mas and pas, practically climbing on them with fear. Some bawled louder than anything. He looked like something right out of a western movie.

Luke usually stopped at the feed store to order corn chop or block salt. Then he might pick up his money at the

creamery and maybe buy two or three pairs of overalls at
Mercer's. Once in a while he'd pause at the grocery store to
pick up some canned peaches or ring bologna. The clerks
scampered around to get his things and package them so
he would get, and get fast. Kids stood around, their noses
pressed to the window, watching his every move.

The bottom line was that every man, woman, and child,
and even the law was shoe-shaking scared of Luke Webster.
They just left him entirely alone and breathed a sigh of relief
when he'd get back on his gelding and ride out of town.

Luke never did anything real bad that I know of. Some
said his sister, Anna, was really afraid of him, but I'm not so
sure. One time when I was in Peterson's on Valentine's Day,
he came in and bought one of those big, sweet-smelling
boxes of candy tied with a big red bow. It had to be for Anna.

Anyway, it was always a whole lot of excitement when
Luke came to town. Most of us waited to see him ride in.
It was better than the movies.

"He's coming! He's coming!" Troop yelled. "Come on,
Carley, Luke is coming to town."

I looked up from hoeing the potatoes. I was willing to
use any excuse to take a breather. "Is he coming in his
truck or on his horse?" I asked, wiping the sweat away
with my bandana.

"He's riding his horse! Come on or you'll miss him."

I looked down at the rows of potatoes I had yet to hoe. I
squished my face all up, trying to think what I'd better do.
"I'd better stick around and finish this. Ma said not to go
anywhere until this patch was done."

"Come on, Carley," Troop coaxed. "When we get back
I'll help you finish. You'll be done faster in the long run."

I shook my head. Dog-gone if Troop couldn't always
give the best reasons. He could argue anyone out of anything and he knew it.

"You've got to come today, especially. They say something's the matter with him."

I put the hoe handle under my arm and looked at Troop. "What're you talking about? Everyone knows that there's always been something wrong with Luke Webster for years and years."

Troop shook his head. "No. I don't mean that. There's something else wrong with him. He's got his shotgun strapped to his saddle and he's headed right toward town. Some people say he's after someone. Maybe someone who tried to cheat him or something."

I looked toward town and down again at the potatoes—back and forth, back and forth. Finally, I shrugged, throwing down my hoe.

Troop smiled. He knew he'd won again. I only hoped Ma didn't come outside to check until I got back.

Troop and I ran as fast as we could to get to our favorite spot. We had a place high up in an old oak tree right next to the street. Luke couldn't see us but we had a great view of him.

My sides felt as if they were going to split when we got to the tree. It made me mad when I noticed Troop was hardly breathing. He always could out run me. Dog-gone him anyway.

Troop pointed down the street and started climbing up the tree faster than a chimpanzee. I followed him until we both got to our favorite limb high above the street. We looked down the street through the parted branches. Only a few people were out. Most of them had run to get into stores. Some jumped in their trucks and cars, high-tailing it out of town. Luke Webster was no one to fool with. Only a few dimwitted old ones still walked around as if nothing was about to happen.

"Look how crazy those people are. They act as if nothing is happening. They must not know about Luke Webster," Troop said, pointing down to a few old guys resting on a bench near the town square.

"They know all right," I said in a tone of wisdom. "But,

when you get that old you're not afraid any more. After all, your time is coming anyway."

Troop nodded. "Yeah, you're probably right."

"Here he comes!" I said to Troop. "I can see him about three blocks away. There's not a bike, truck, or car on the streets. It's as if he's got the whole town to himself except for Sheriff Parsons." I pointed at the square where the sheriff sat waiting in his car for Luke to do his business and leave.

"We'd better be quiet now," I said. "I sure don't want him to see us up here. Especially now that he's got a gun."

Troop and I watched Luke sit astride his horse, looking straight ahead. His beard blew back from his waist. He was as big as a mountain on that horse. The gelding walked slowly up the hill toward town. I looked around, spotting a lot of people peeking through venetian blinds and curtains at him coming toward the square. A few kids hid behind barrels and garbage cans, watching him.

"He looks like something right out of a John Wayne movie," Troop said in a gasp.

"Yeah, he's bigger than anything I've seen in a movie."

Luke was so close Troop and I heard the gelding's hoof-beats and heard it snort. Luke looked straight ahead, not blinking an eye. And then he pulled up his reins right beside where Troop and I were hidden in that tree. Leaning forward, he pulled his shotgun out of his saddle. Troop and I held our breaths. We thought we might be dropping from that tree at any minute.

Luke looked up and spotted us hiding behind those branches. He eyed us for several seconds. I melted beneath those black eyes looking out from under the brim of that hat. He never said a word. He just looked at us, perched up there too afraid to swallow or breathe.

After what seemed like a year he turned away, starting on down the street. With one hand, he pushed the stock of the shotgun under his armpit and fired. The gelding reared and came down snorting. Luke fired again.

36

I heard a few women scream, a few men cuss, and a whole lot of kids start to bawl. Troop and I sat there, our legs dangling in mid-air, waiting, not knowing if the next blast was going to pop us out of the tree or not.

Luke kept the gun beneath his arm and moved on up the street. After about a hundred steps he pulled in the reins and shot twice again. This time he shouted real loud.

The shout gave me the shivers because it sounded almost like a woman's scream it was so shrill. Finally, Luke reloaded and went on up the hill. Just as he got by the corner of Peterson's, he turned in the saddle and fired two shots at the big front window. The glass shattered and tinkled to the sidewalk. I think I heard Mrs. Peterson from the back room.

Luke stood there just as straight as could be for quite some time. Finally, he shot once in the air, rammed his gelding in the flanks, and charged around the square, firing as he went. Four old men looked up from their checker game and then back down as he rode past them. Before you could say "Jack Robinson" he passed us in the tree and was high-tailing it back out of town.

Troop looked at me, his eyes so wide I thought they were going to pop out of his head. I looked over to Sheriff Parsons' car and saw his head stick up from the back seat. He put on his siren and screeched his tires as he started down the street chasing Luke.

That night at supper I felt the tension in the room. Pa forked in his fried potatoes, nudging at his mustache when some caught in it. Ma looked at me and then at him. Finally, she spoke.

"Did a good job hoeing those potatoes today, Carley."

"Thanks, Ma," I answered. "I'll do the rest of it tomorrow."

"Yes, that would be nice," she replied.

Pa nodded, poking his fork into his piece of meat.

"Your Ma tells me you took off before you got the patch all hoed today. Is that right?"

I looked over at Ma. Her eyes told me I was caught like a rat in a trap. I never could get anything past her except maybe crawling out the window the other night to go to Cave Springs. Down deep I know she'll find that one out too, someday. It was only a matter of time. I nodded. "Yes, I did. But Troop and I came back to finish most of it later. We probably got a lot more done than if I stayed and did it all alone," I argued.

Pa's heavy eyebrows lowered over his eyes. I knew that look all too well. "That's not the point," he said. "When your Ma tells you something, you do it. I don't want you high-tailing it when you're supposed to stay around and do your chores. You disobeyed and that's that."

"I looked out there and I didn't know where you were," she said. "And...and then I heard those gunshot blasts coming from town. I didn't know what to think."

I saw that Ma was pale around the lips. I knew she was either scared or real mad. Tonight, maybe it was a little or a lot of each.

"Tonight, you'll go on to bed right after supper," he said.

"Ah, Pa," I whined. "My favorite radio shows are on tonight. I never miss them."

"Tonight, you'll miss them," he said sternly.

"Ah, gee," I said, poking at my potatoes.

"You did a real foolish thing leaving and going up town," he said.

"Troop just wanted me to see Luke Webster coming in to town. We always go up there when he comes to town. We had no way of knowing that he'd go crazy today."

"You're just lucky you weren't shot or killed or something," Ma said, tears welling in her eyes.

Pa turned and looked down at me. "Carley, that's when bad things happen. Times when you disobey like that."

"Luke didn't hurt nobody," I argued. "He just shot

down the street a few times and shot out Peterson's window, that's all."

"Sheriff Parsons and some of the boys followed Luke all over town. He took that big buckskin through yards, driveways, and vacant lots. He went through gardens and flower beds. That big horse about smashed every living plant in Belford. At last they cornered him in Dooley's garage, that horse lathering and frothing at the mouth."

"Where's he at now?" I asked.

"He's up town in the jail. He'll be there until tomorrow morning when some of the county boys are coming over to Belford and taking him back to the County Seat."

"What happened?" I asked. "Luke never did anything like that before? What happened to him this time?"

"Nobody knows," Pa said. "They went out to tell Anna about it so she could send some clothes for him and such and...and..."

Pa paused and I knew something wasn't quite right.

"And what, Pa? What were you going to say?"

"And they found Anna Webster dead in her bed. The poor old lady had a heart attack and died during the night, the coroner said."

Ma put her fingers to her lips but no sound came out.

Pa looked down at his plate and laid his fork on it.

I sat there a little while, looking down at the floor. Pretty soon I asked to be excused to my room. I didn't feel like listening to the radio tonight anyway.

That night I must've laid on my bed two or three hours just thinking about Luke Webster and his sister, Anna. I wondered what would happen to him now. Would they take him away for good? How would he get along without his older sister? She was the one who took care of him since he was a little kid.

My thoughts got all mixed up. I wondered why God would let something like that happen. It was just like the time I had this pet rabbit named Droopy, because his ears drooped so much. He was a real special pet. I loved him more than anything. He was one of the healthiest rabbits you'd ever want to meet. But one morning I went out to feed him some lettuce and carrots and stuff from Pa's store, and he was laying in the bottom of his cage, stone dead. He wasn't sick or anything the day before. He wasn't old or anything...he just died. I never could understand it. It's kind of like this happening. I don't understand it at all. I suppose only God really understands it.

Something hit my window. It plunked and then plunked again. I got up and looked out down below. In the shadows, I saw Troop throwing pebbles at my window to wake me. The thing was, I wasn't even asleep. I couldn't sleep tonight at all. Carefully, I hauled the window up and stretched my head out.

"What is it, Troop? What do you want, anyway?" I asked.

He half-hollered, half-whispered. "Carley, get the slat out of your bed and come on."

"What for? It's after eleven o'clock. I know because I just checked my pocketwatch."

"Yeah, it's about that time," he answered. "I thought maybe you and I could go up to the jail and peek in and get a good look at Luke Webster before they take him away tomorrow."

"What? You must be crazy!"

Troop put his hands on his hips in disgust. "What does that mean? You don't want to see him close up or what?"

"That ain't it. I just don't see me pulling out the slat to my bed, putting it in the crotch of that old elm, and climbing across just to go up town to see Luke Webster."

"Well, I see you doing it," Troop argued.

I tightened my belly muscles because I knew Troop was about ready to talk me into something again. I shook my head. "I don't know. I'm in trouble as it is. I got sent to bed tonight because you talked me in to going up to see

Luke before I finished hoeing the potatoes. I didn't get to hear any of my radio programs tonight."

"So, you're saying you don't want to see Luke, right?"

"I didn't say I didn't want to see him. I just don't want to get into more trouble. That razor strap of Pa's hasn't been used for awhile and I just as soon keep it that way. Besides, Luke Webster is dangerous."

"What could he do to us?" Troop asked with a shrug. "He's locked in tighter than a drum behind bars. There isn't anything he can do to us."

I stopped and thought for a few moments. Troop was right. Luke Webster couldn't do anything to us from his jail cell.

"If you don't want to come that's up to you. I know I'm going up to get a look. His window is in the alley behind the pool hall. All we have to do is get a couple of boxes and we can see straight into his cell. And there isn't a darn thing he can do about it." Troop sighed. "Do you want to go or not? I'm not waiting out here forever. I'll get one of the other Mustangs to go."

I shook my head. I knew I was hooked. "All right. Hold your horses. It's going to take me a few minutes to get dressed and get that slat out from under my bed."

Before I knew it I was down beside Troop and we were running through the back alleys toward town. We didn't want to be on the sidewalks for fear someone would spot us and wonder what we were doing up town this time of night. Only a few lights burned. It was so dark in the alley that one time we tripped over a garbage can spilling everything out. It made more noise than a Chinese New Year. I was afraid every house in the neighborhood would light up and we'd be hauled in. We crouched in the shadows as one light popped on and a man in his pajamas stepped out back with a bat or something in his hand. He looked out at the alley from one end to the other. Finally, I heard his wife ask him something and he replied: "Naw...just some cussed cat or dog."

Troop and I started breathing again and tiptoeing our way on up town, being more careful this time.

"Here it is," Troop said, nodding toward the small barred window on the brick jailhouse.

"That window is over eight feet high. We're going to need something to climb on or we're not going to be able to see nothing," I said.

Troop spotted two crates somebody threw away. Before you knew it, he dragged those crates up next to the wall piling one on top of the other.

"You want to go first or do you want me to?" he asked.

"I'll take a look first," I said. Hitching up my overalls, I started climbing up on the crates. They wobbled from side to side. "Hey, keep them steady, will you," I whispered. "They could give way and I'd fall flat."

"I've got them. Don't worry," Troop whispered back.

I got my balance and stood there for a moment, wondering if I should do what I planned to do. We could be caught window peeping or something. I was sure that was a crime in itself. We both could be spending time in that cell next to old Luke. The thought of it sent goosebumps racing down my back.

There wasn't a sound anywhere except for crickets chirping and a dog barking in the distance every now and then. I raised to my tiptoes and looked through the metal bars into the cell. A dim light filtered into the cell from the other room. I knew someone was in the other room, probably sleeping.

"See anything?" Troop whispered.

I waited a few moments until my eyes were better adjusted. "Nothing but his bed," I said.

"Look again. He's in there. It's a small cell. The Sheriff showed it to me once. There's nowhere he can go. He's got to be in there."

"I looked again. My eyes went from one corner of the room to the other. I still just saw his cot; nothing else. I turned, looking down at Troop. "I don't see nothing except his bed."

"That can't be," Troop said. "Get down and let me have a look."

"Now, wait a minute. Let me take one last look. You'll get your chance. Remember, it was you who came and got me tonight. Let me have one more chance," I pleaded.

Troop sighed. He grabbed hold of the crates for a tighter hold. I stood on tiptoe, pressing my nose through the bars of the dark cell. I felt it before I saw anything. It was someone's hot breath flowing into my face. Suddenly, I was looking right into the black eyes of Luke Webster. I could even feel a slight tickle from his bushy beard. He looked at me for several seconds and I stood there unable to move a muscle. Suddenly, he opened his bearded mouth and screamed. It was that same high-pitched scream that he did in town today; the one that sends icy chills running down your back. It was real high and shrill. It sounded like someone scraping their fingernails on a blackboard. Gasping, I reared back.

Troop grunted, pushing the crates together. It did no good. I lunged back and fell. The crates came crashing down on top of me. The screams went on and on.

Troop and I bolted to our feet, turning tail as fast as jackrabbits down the alley, knocking over garbage cans in the dark every few feet. Lights came on all over town as the screams went on and on like something eerie from the grave.

Chapter 5

The day I found old Shiner was really something. It was so hot you could pop corn right on the sidewalk. Troop and I decided to take our poles and go down to Turtle Creek for some serious fishing. We knew a hole down there that had the fattest, wiggliest bullheads known to man. You just put a grasshopper or a grub on your hook and faster than you could shake a stick a bullhead would pull your line clear down to the bottom. That cork would take a real nose dive. I laid there close to the bank, dangling my toes in the warm water. Today, I wore a straw hat. The sun filtered through an old weeping willow, landing on my chest and legs. I had the hat over my eyes. There hadn't been one bit of action on my line for over an hour. Troop and I both guessed it was because it was just too blamed hot.

I laid there smelling the clover, asters, and goldenrod in the air. Those old bullheads must be deep today and swimming on the bottom in cooler water. My brain got real heavy and I felt myself slip in and out of sleep a lot like the old men dozing on the town square on summer afternoons. Every once in a while I'd open my eyes and swing my hat at a bunch of pesky mosquitoes. I'd just get all comfortable-like, my back pressed against the cool mud bank, and they'd come again. It sure made me mad.

Looking over, I saw Troop grinning out of the corner of my eye. He looked pure Indian today. I guess it was because of the hawk feather he found on the way out and stuck in his black, shoulder-length hair. His skin was the color of toast and his eyes looked like two pieces of coal.

"Those pesky mosquitoes!" I yelled, swinging my hat at them again.

"They aren't bothering me. I just lay here and they don't bother me at all."

He was laying there, one leg propping up the other, his foot sort of dancing up and down.

It wasn't hard to figure, I thought. Indians are meant to live in nature, out of doors. God probably made them so insects, hot weather, cold, or rain doesn't bother them none. Troop never seemed to get as cold, hot, or wet as I did. And bugs never bothered him. He was laying there just as contented as a baby. "Do you ever miss South Dakota, Troop?" I asked. I don't know why I blurted that out all of a sudden. It just came out. Troop nudged up the brim of his hat, uncovering an eye.

"No," he said simply.

A one word answer never did satisfy me. "Why not?" I asked. I saw that the question put a lot of thoughts in his mind all at the same time. His lips drew tight and his jaw sort of clenched. Muscles jumped beneath his right eye.

"I didn't like it on the reservation." He picked up a rock and threw it into the water. "My father wasn't a man there."

Propping myself up on my elbow, I looked at him thoughtfully. "What do you mean, not a man?"

"He lived a useless life," he replied. "He had no job, no dignity. He drank an awful lot. Sometimes he acted real crazy." He looked over and winked slyly. "You know what they say about Indians and firewater?"

"Yeah, I guess so." I really didn't.

"Now, he works and brings home money from the railroad. We have plenty of food for everyone. And he doesn't drink anymore. Everything is much better."

I nodded. I knew that Charlie Whitewater, with his felt derby and his black braids hanging down to his waist, was one of the most honorable and hard working men in town. It was hard for me to believe that he was ever anything else.

Picking up a flat stone, I skipped it across the creek. It made three not-so-bad skips before it sank out of sight. I looked over at Troop, grinning with pride.

Troop laughed, picking up a flat rock. With a flick of his wrist, he threw it and it made five perfect skips before it sank.

I sighed. It seemed to me he could always do everything better. I was used to it by now. "Did you ever have a pet, Troop?" I asked.

Troop skimmed another rock across the water. "Once, I had a dog in South Dakota."

"What was his name?" I asked.

"He didn't have a name. None of the dogs on the reservation had names."

"What ever happened to him? Why didn't you bring him when you left South Dakota?"

"Because one winter we had no food and we had to eat him."

I looked over at Troop and gulped. "You...you ate your dog?"

Troop nodded. "Yes. That's why no one names their dogs. In case the winter gets real bad and people are hungry, then the dog must go in the stew pot. We had to have something to feed the family. It was either that or we all would starve. Many people had to do it."

My belly started to bounce around. "I...I suppose you had to do it," I said, swallowing hard.

"Yes. We had to do it," he said simply.

"Ma and Pa promised me I could have a dog one of these days. I can't wait. I've wanted one for years."

"You name him, Carley. You name him because he'll never go into the stew pot."

I nodded, looking over at my cork floating lazily on the top of the water. "They just aren't biting today. It's too hot. There probably won't be any action until the sun goes down."

"They've all gone to deeper waters. You're right about that," Troop said.

"What say we leave our poles here and go up the creek a ways and explore?"

"You know every inch of Turtle Creek, Carley."

"Well, I'm not going to just lay here and wilt. Do you want to go or not?"

"Might as well," Troop said, jamming his pole further into the bank for safe keeping. "There won't be any fish biting until it cools off."

Troop and I left our poles and started following Turtle Creek. One time we followed it for miles until it emptied into the Big Blue River. I thought we'd never come to the end of it. The mouth was wide and deep.

Troop and I could always think of things to talk about. It was great to be free and to be a kid growing up in Belford, Kansas. I couldn't imagine growing up in a city all crowded and smoky. I'd seen films on it at the free picture show on Saturdays. I saw New York and Pittsburgh and places like that with their tall buildings and crowded tenements. There wasn't any grass or trees in sight. It made me shiver to think what growing up there was like. God had been right nice to me, I had to admit.

"Hey, look up ahead!" Troop said, in a half-whisper. "A blue heron!"

I followed his point. For a few moments I thought it was just his imagination. It looked like a pile of sticks. But Troop was right. There was a blue heron standing in a shallow place in the creek. It looked real graceful-like and pretty. We crept closer and closer.

A stick cracked beneath my feet and the sound made the heron take flight. Troop always walked better than me. The blue heron raised right out of the water and flew up into the sky. It was a very pretty sight.

"Sorry about that. I must've tripped on a root or something." Troop didn't reply. I don't think it mattered to him one bit.

We walked on. Big, bulgy-eyed bullfrogs plopped into

the water at the edge of the bank. Some of them weighed about two pounds. One time Troop and I caught one and caught flies for it to eat. It got all skinny and we found out later that a bullfrog won't eat bugs you catch for it. It only eats flies and insects in motion. That seems real strange to me. We did all the work for it.

Troop and I walked on, watching some pack rats work on their house in a tree laying across the creek and a mud hen streak across the water.

The trees lining the water made it real nice and shady. A little breeze swept across the creek, fanning our sweaty skins and making us feel a whole lot cooler. "Watch out!" I yelled. For once I saw something before he did.

Troop stopped in midstep and froze like a statue. On the ground, in front of us, was an Osage Copperhead, all coiled up, his tongue flicking in and out smelling us.

"Don't move, Carley. If you move, he may strike. He's poisonous so we'd better take it real slow and easy."

My mouth got as dry as cotton. That copperhead weaved about, smelling us with his tongue. His head danced and bobbed and his nose bumped into Troop's leg. Troop never moved a muscle. Sweat dripped off my face and down my back. My thoughts went back to Bill Wiley, a friend of mine, who got bit by a copperhead and was in a coma for five days last summer. He finally pulled through but everyone in town prayed all night for him.

Troop and I stood there, barely breathing. That old copperhead waited, bobbing his head not six inches from our legs. I don't think Troop batted an eye, flexed a muscle, or even swallowed. He was as still as a tree. The copperhead's tongue brushed my leg once and I nearly hollered, but I choked it back. Its little black beady eyes watched me closely. Finally, it lowered its head, fell to the ground, and slithered off. I took a breath, wiping off the sweat pouring down my face.

"Whew!" I said. "That was too close."

"I know," Troop said. "But it was smart to outwait the Osage. Any sudden movement and we'd have been bit for sure."

I nodded, believing Troop's every word. That's something he knew a whole lot about, nature and God's creatures living there.

Troop and I kept on walking, not saying a whole lot after our close call with the Osage copperhead. We kept close to the bank because the cool mud felt good on the soles of our feet. We skipped rocks, chased a few bullfrogs, tried to seine some minnows with a gunny sack we found—things like that. Anyway, we must've walked four or five miles along Turtle Creek that scorcher of an afternoon.

Troop stopped. Pulling off his straw hat, he cocked his head to one side just like a wild animal that senses danger or something. I stopped in my tracks beside him. Whenever Troop does something like that, I always figure it's something pretty important. He cocked his head to the other side now. His long, straight hair blew in the breeze. His eyes got all glazed over, he was concentrating so hard.

"What is it?" I asked, about ready to bust with curiosity. "Why're you all tensed up?"

Troop waved his hand to quiet me and went on listening. Finally, his eyes went out to a pile of sticks and limbs sticking out over the water. It looked like part of a beaver dam half washed away. His nostrils wrinkled, smelling the air.

"There's something in that pile of brush over there, Carley. I can hear something," he said.

"Probably a beaver or a pack rat," I said staring at the pile of brush.

"Could be," Troop said. "But, it doesn't smell like that. It's got a sharper smell."

I whiffed the air. I couldn't smell a thing except the stink of the creek mud.

Carefully, Troop walked forward, one easy step after another. His eyes moved back and forth.

"Better be careful. It might be a water moccasin or a bull snake, Troop," I warned. "Better take a stick with you."

Troop never paid any attention. He walked directly to the pile of brush.

I stood there watching him, barely breathing. I thought I just about had enough excitement for one afternoon already. "What is it?" I whispered. "Did you find anything?"

Troop bent clear over and looked into the dark shadows of the brush pile. "Come on over, Carley. I found what was making the noise."

I ran forward. I could trust Troop. Had it been Mick telling me to take a look at something, I would've been a whole lot more careful. You couldn't trust Mick Fuller that was for sure. "What is it? What're you being so mysterious about?" I asked.

Troop smiled. "Look what we got here, would you, Carley?"

Leaning down, I peered into the shadows of that brush pile. The blackest eyes I ever saw were staring back at me. The critter was all wet and hunched up. It was shaking real bad. Its eyes were wild with fear.

"It's a raccoon," Troop said, getting to his knees.

I frowned. "I know it's a raccoon, for criminy sakes. I can tell that."

"The poor thing's caught in a trap. Somebody forgot to pick this trap up after this winter."

"He's sure skinny," I said. "No telling how long he's been in there."

"Look!" Troop said, pointing. "He's bleeding badly."

"He's caught by his hind foot," I said looking up at Troop.

Troop shook his head in sympathy.

I got down beside him and took a closer look. "Poor thing," I whispered beneath my breath. "The poor thing."

"We probably should put him out of his misery, Carley."

Swinging my head around, I looked at Troop with disbelief. "Are you saying what I think you're saying? Are you saying we should kill him?"

Troop lowered his voice as if he didn't want to let the raccoon hear him. "He's suffering, Carley. We can't just leave him there to starve to death."

"I know that." I turned back and looked at the raccoon again. "I suppose he was close enough to the water to drink. I'll bet he hasn't had anything to eat for a long time."

"It isn't right to let him suffer." Troop got to his feet and looked around the bank. He picked up a piece of stout drift wood and walked back to the brush pile.

I looked at him, but I couldn't speak for some reason. My throat felt all clogged. Troop noticed how bad I felt.

"You know it's the only thing we can do, don't you, Carley? He'll die a slow death this way."

I nodded, still unable to speak. I knew Troop would never kill a creature unless it was for survival or to stop its suffering. That was the kind of person he was. He had a great respect and love for God's creatures.

Troop walked toward the animal. The raccoon sensed the great danger. He ran back and forth, jerking on the chain that held the jaws of the trap. My face wrinkled every time the chain stopped him. I imagined the fierce pain he was going through. Troop stopped and raised the heavy branch over his head. I saw tears bank in his eyes. The raccoon's eyes met Troop's and the animal froze on his hind legs, waiting for the end.

Troop took a deep breath, tensing, ready to let the branch fall.

"Stop! Don't do it!" I yelled. Troop turned, frowning. He wanted to get it over with. "Don't kill him. I want him. I'll take him home and fix his hind leg. He can be just like a dog. Ma and Pa said I could have a dog soon."

Troop lowered the branch. "You can't take him home, Carley."

"And why not? He'd be just as good as a dog. Ma and Pa wouldn't care."

"You can't pen up wild animals. It's against nature. They have feelings and instincts that Manito has given them. They must always return to the wild."

I decided not to listen to Troop.

"He's almost crazy with pain, Carley. After this he'd never trust any human. He'll probably die, he's so weak. He's too far gone now. Look how sick he looks." He pointed.

I looked at the coon's face. It had two furry black circles around his eyes. Those eyes looked right at me and I melted. "I still want to try. I still want to get Shiner out of the trap."

"What'd you call him?"

"Shiner." I grinned. "That would make a real good name for him. He looks like he's got two shiners around his eyes."

Troop threw the branch into the creek in disgust. But I don't really think he was disgusted at all. In fact, I think he was relieved that he didn't have to kill the raccoon. He just wanted to act like what I wanted was impossible.

"How are we going to get him out of the trap? Just tell me that," he asked, his hands on his hips.

I knew I had to think real fast. My brain started spinning. "Well...well, couldn't you sort of tease him with a stick? You know, wave it in front of his face. While you're doing that, I could creep up from behind and work on that trap. Once I get it open, I'll grab his hind leg and you can..." I paused because I knew that animal would bite hard to protect himself.

Troop smiled. "And then I can take this gunny sack we've been using for seining minnows and drop it over his head. Is that what you were going to say?"

I nodded. "That's it! That's exactly what I was going to say."

Troop shook his head and laughed. "You must want that coon pretty bad to risk some good bites and scratches from him. Remember, he's half-crazy from pain and starvation now. He thinks we're out to kill him. He's going to fight us with all the strength he has left."

"I know it, Troop. But, we've got to give it a try. It's either that or he'll die anyway."

"Yeah, I suppose you're right," Troop said.

I breathed deep. I knew he'd help me now. I looked around and ran after the wet gunny sack and a stick. "Here, take this and wave it in front of his nose. He'll stand up and jerk the chain tight. I'll work up behind him and open the trap." Troop nodded, taking the stick. He pushed the gunny sack into his back pocket.

I waited until Troop got real close to the coon. He waved the stick in front of its face and it swung and swiped at it with its sharp claws like it was the enemy. I got down on all fours and crawled toward the brush pile. The creek water bobbed beneath me.

The raccoon was standing up on its hind legs, making a hissing sound kind of like a cat. Its mouth was open and I saw the rows of sharp teeth flashing in the sun. I wobbled for a second and almost fell head first into the creek, but then caught my balance and went on getting as close to the trap as I could.

Troop kept on waving the stick in front of the coon's nose and yelling. Now and then he'd tap him on the head and the coon would rear back and hiss at him.

Sweat poured off my chin. It ran into my eyes and stung like salt. I licked a layer of sweat off my upper lip. Reaching out, I carefully took hold of the jaws of the steel trap. I knew I was going to have to work fast. Once the coon's foot was free, I was going to have to grab him fast before he turned and bit me. I hoped that Troop had the gunny sack ready to throw over him. If he didn't, I knew I'd be in for a bunch of real hurtful bites.

I glanced at Troop and nodded. This was the time for action. The coon stretched the chain to its limit to bat at the stick Troop was waving. Quickly, I reached in with both hands and grunted as I wrenched open the tight jaws of the trap. It was a real tough spring, but it budged just enough for the animal to slip its foot out. In an instant, I had hold of his hind leg.

The coon was confused. It didn't even try to run. Maybe it was because it had lost so much blood and it was so weak from starvation that he couldn't, I don't know. It seemed more like he was just real confused. I was just ready to yell when I saw Troop flying forward with the gunny sack wide open. Before you could say "Jack Robinson", that old coon was in the bag and Troop had him above his head in victory.

"I got him! I got him, Carley!" Troop hollered.

I ran over and patted Troop on the back. "Good work. Real good work." I took the twisted sack out of his hands and lowered it gently to the bank. The bag jumped and jounced all over the place.

The raccoon hissed and squealed inside. Carefully, I opened the top and peered down into it. The raccoon looked straight up at me half with fear and half with hatred.

"Well, what do you think of your new dog, Carley?" Troop asked, laughing.

"He's just fine," I answered, twisting the top shut. "Let's get going. We've got a long way to go to get our poles. Besides, I want to get Shiner home so I can start to fix his leg."

Chapter 6

"Think that poultice will help with the swelling, Ma? He sure looks sick-like. His ears are down and his eyes are wet around them."

Ma swept back grey wisps of hair and frowned. I could tell she was taking the matter real serious. She shook her head. "I don't know, Carley. You're right, he does look sick. The poor thing has been caught in that trap for so long, it's no wonder he's half-dead. It's the Lord's miracle that he didn't die from bleeding to death." She studied the hurt leg for a few seconds.

"The poultice should draw out the infection, but there's no way of telling."

I scratched one of his ears affectionately. He looked up and tried to bare his teeth. He had a hard time because I had twine wrapped around his muzzle to keep his mouth shut. It was either that or get the daylights bitten out of me. I did feel a little sorry for him, though. He really looked helpless.

Ma tied a clean bandage around his bloody foot.

She looked up, smiling. "I know you want to keep this animal, Carley. But you still have to ask your Pa. You know how he feels about keeping anything wild. He's always said that God made them to run wild and its sacrilegious to pen or tie them up." She shook her head. "I wouldn't get your hopes up too high. He might have you take Shiner back out by the creek and turn him loose."

"I know how Pa feels about keeping wild animals. And I guess I agree with him about most of it. But, I don't think Shiner can fend for himself. If I turn him loose the way he is now, he'd be prey for some other animal. Or worse yet, he'd starve to death because he's too weak to get his own food. At least Pa might let me keep him long enough to nurse him back to health. Don't you think?"

Ma hunched her shoulders. "I'm not answering for your Pa. He'll have to do that for himself. It could be that the animal is so hurt and scared that he'll never trust a human. He's been in pain and terrified too long. He may never tame down. And I don't want you bit up, young man." Her voice was hard.

"I'm not taking any chances, Ma. Troop and I both came close to having his teeth in us. I'm going to take it real slow and maybe I can get him to trust me. It'll take a long time, I know that, but maybe it'll happen someday."

"That's if and when your Pa lets you keep him." Carefully, she lifted Shiner off the table and handed him to me. "Now, take him out to the rabbit hutch. Take the muzzle off him and leave him something to eat. He'll probably pull that bandage off, but by now the poultice has done some good, if it's ever going to." She looked at me. "And I want you to get some wood for the cook stove and feed the chickens. You've spent half the day tending to this animal."

I knew by the sound of her voice she wasn't asking; she was telling. I took hold of Shiner real careful-like and started to the door. "I will, Ma. I'll do it right away." Just then I thought of something. "Oh, yeah, thanks a whole lot for helping Shiner. I really appreciate it and I know he does, too."

"No more talk about that animal, now. You just get and get those chores done." She pointed her finger at me, but I could tell she wasn't all that stern.

"Right away, Ma. Right away," I said. I walked to Droopy's old hutch, now to be Shiner's new home. Carefully, I opened the mesh wire door, laid him down easily, and nimbly pulled the twine from his muzzle. Right away, he lunged toward the back of the cage. He turned around, baring his teeth and stood on his hind legs. He made a hissing sound as though he dared me to touch him.

"There, Shiner, you're going to be okay," I said quietly.

"Just calm down. Ma and me just want to help you, that's all. We just want to get you well."

I don't think what I said made any difference to him. He stayed right there, rearing up on his hind legs, making that sound. I reached in to pet his head. Like lightning, he lunged forward and buried his sharp teeth into my hand. I squealed as loud as a raiding Indian. It surprised me more than it hurt. I was scared when I saw blood oozing out of those little holes his teeth made. I slammed the cage door closed and hooked it. Reaching into my back pocket, I wrapped my handkerchief around my hand.

"Okay," I said, between gritted teeth. "If that's what you want, I'll leave you alone." My face was all hot and red with anger. "You're not showing much gratitude, I can tell you that. You would've died caught in that trap. You should be grateful to me. You've got a strange way of showing it, that's for sure."

Sometimes my head is as hard and as thick as a rock. I should've realized that it was natural for Shiner to be skittish about all humans. After all, it was a human who caused him all his misery in the first place. It was a human who forgot to pick up his trap and nearly caused him to starve to death. I should've thought of all of that, but when a guy gets bit all he knows for a while is that he's real mad.

I tied the handkerchief around my hand tightly and decided not to tell Ma about it. It would be just another reason she'd have for not letting me keep him. And then, sure as the world, Pa would have me take him back to the creek. Nope, I decided, I'd do my best to keep it quiet as long as I could.

I got the chickens fed, chopped kindling for the cook stove, hoed the potatoes, and fixed the wire on Ma's clothes line. So far I managed to keep my hand away from Ma's eyes. Everytime she came close I either put it in my pocket, hid it behind a bunch of wood, or held it behind my back. She was so busy baking, washing and things, she didn't notice. My hand was throbbing a little, but not real bad. Once, I unwrapped it and looked at it. It had stopped bleeding a long time ago and now had a dark crusty look, and my handkerchief had brownish blood stains on it. I knew I'd have to throw that handkerchief away or she'd find out for sure. You can't keep hardly any secrets from Ma.

I crept over to Shiner's cage and looked in at him. I had put a nice soft bed of straw in the bottom and wired two cans to the mesh, for his food and water. I was real happy to see that he had eaten the fish heads I'd given him. All that was left were some white bones and skulls. That was a good sign, I thought.

It was getting close to three o'clock, so I plunked down under a willow with my head cushioned on my arm. It was a lot cooler under there, and I liked to shut my eyes and listen to the light rustle of the willow leaves when they rubbed together in the breeze. Ma had given me a nickel to go to Peterson's for a Green River. She said it was payment for the good work I did today. A Green River would really taste good about now, but I just couldn't muster the energy to get up and get going to town. It was so cool and nice beneath that willow.

My hat was pulled down over my eyes, and all I heard was the willow leaves and a few mosquitoes whining around my head. I scrunched myself into a nice groove on the ground. My eyelids were heavy and I sighed, knowing I was about ready to slip into some sleep. I didn't try fighting it at all. A little shut-eye wouldn't hurt anyone. Besides, it was summer and the chores were done. My time was my own. Boy, I was one lucky kid. This was the way to live.

Just as I dipped into sleep, I felt something poke at my shoulder. Squinting open one eye, I looked down at a dark toe with a ragged, broken nail. I looked on up a rolled pants leg to Troop staring down at me with those black eyes of his. I might have known I wouldn't have heard him slip up on me. It's as though he walked a little ways above the ground. I wished I could do that.

"What you waking a guy up for, Troop?" I asked. "Can't you see that I'm plum tuckered out? I fed the chickens, chopped kindling, and hoed about a mile and a half of garden. What's so important that you've got to get me up, anyway?"

Troop stared down at me. The wind whipped his shoulder-length hair. His eyes sparkled from beneath the brim of his hat.

"They're back in town, Carley. There's five wagons this time. They're camped out across the river bridge. They've got a campfire going and everything. They must have at least thirty horses tied together."

"You talking about the gypsy band? They back again, in the same spot?" I asked.

"Yeah. They've been stopping at farms trying to sell their horses. Some won't buy them, you know. Some people say they're stolen. I've been up there watching them. There's a whole bunch of kids up there just standing around watching them go about their business. You want to go up and take a look?" he asked.

"I've seen them before. They'll stay about two days and then they'll go on to another town. There's really nothing to see."

"Yeah, but these are real gypsies. Nomads, my parents call them. It's fun to watch them."

I sat up, stretched, and groaned all at the same time. "I don't know, Troop. Ma gave me a nickel for a Green River at Peterson's and I can tell you I didn't even have the energy to go up there to get one. And you know how I love Green Rivers." I yawned. "So what makes you think I'd want to go way past town and over the river bridge to watch a bunch of gypsies?"

"No reason, I guess. Except Mick and his gang are there. They've been giving those people a hard time. He's been calling them names and everything. Some of his gang are throwing rocks at them."

"Sheriff Parsons will take care of Mick and his gang if he keeps it up."

Troop shook his head. "I wouldn't be so sure about that. You know how the Sheriff feels about those people. He's real glad when they leave each year. You know people say they steal, put curses on people and crops, and even kidnap children. Some of the kids' parents don't want them around them at all."

"Yeah, I know. Ma and Pa always warned me to be careful when they came to town. Some parents won't let their kids out of their sight when they're around."

Troop sighed real heavy, placing his hands on his hips. "Well, make up your mind. Do you want to go out there and see what's going on, or are you just going to lay there and sleep the rest of the day?"

I sighed, and pushed myself to my feet. "All right, all right. I'll go. If I don't, you'll pester me until I do," I muttered.

"You going to tell your Ma?" Troop asked.

"Are you kidding? She would stop me for sure. I'm going on up town as though I'm going up to get my Green River." I thought for a moment. "And I just might get me one while I'm up there. But then I might mosey on up past the river bridge and have a look at that band of gypsies camped there."

Troop threw his head back, laughing. "You're a sly one, Carley. You sure are. You're as slick as an oiled snake."

I thought for a moment. I didn't know if I liked that description or not.

Troop looked down at my bandaged hand. "What you got your hand all wrapped up for?"

"Shiner bit me. Ma and I doctored him up, and when I took the twine off his muzzle, he let me have it when I tried to pet him."

"You should have known enough not to try to pet him for a while, Carley. He's still scared and doesn't trust people at all. It'll take time to get him to trust you."

I looked at my hand. "Yeah, I know. I'll be more careful next time, that's for sure."

Troop placed his arm around my shoulder. "Come on, let's get going. That's a long walk clear out there to the river bridge."

"You're right, Troop." I pointed across the river. "There's Mick and the Spiders. I can see Lowell from here, with his white hair. And I can see Devil standing there like a big lion."

"Yeah. They're giving the gypsies a hard time. Mick's always showing off when his gang's around."

Mick turned around just as we got off the bridge. His hat was pulled low and those beady grey eyes peered out from beneath it.

"What you doing here, Bimberg? Always nosing in where you don't belong as usual."

I shrugged. "I've got just as much right being here as you, Mick. Besides, it's a free country."

"It's a free country all right unless you're talking about gypsies. They don't have any right being here. Every year I give them a hard time and every year they're back. They just don't get the hint."

"They're not hurting anyone. Why don't you just leave them alone," I replied.

Mick stepped up to me, his staff in one hand. Devil followed along his right leg. "You telling me to get, Bimberg?" His thin lips pulled back in a sneer, showing his tobacco stained teeth. "Nobody tells Mick Fuller what to do. I thought you knew that by now."

He looked down into my face. He was so close I felt his hot breath.

"I'm just saying that you can stand here and watch them without giving them a hard time. They aren't hurting anyone."

"Yeah, says you. My Pa told me how they steal from everybody. Last year when they left we didn't have rain here for over a month and the corn burned up. The creeks dried up and the fish died. After that a bunch of farmers' cows dried up and gave no milk." He looked closer. "And, Mr. Big Shot, who do you think made all of those things happen?"

I met him eye to eye. "And you're saying that the gypsies put curses on everyone. Is that what you're saying, Mick?"

"That's exactly what I'm saying.. It all happened just when they left town. They've got evil powers, I tell you. Any ninny knows that." He picked up a rock in the road and hurled it into the gypsies' encampment. The rock ricocheted off one of the caravans. One of the male gypsies peeked out from the caravan and shouted at Mick. It was too far to hear what he said. But I knew he was red-hot mad.

The horses were loosely tied together so they could graze on the soft grasses in the encampment. They were beautiful: Arabians, appaloosas, and palaminoes. They snorted nervously as the rock bounced to the ground.

"You'd better be careful, Mick," I warned. "They may put a curse on you."

"I'd like to see them try it," he sneered. "Right, boys?" he yelled to his gang.

Frank, Lowell, and the rest nodded, calling out in support.

"Look!" someone yelled.

Everyone crowded together to watch. A man, wearing a bright red turban, sat near the campfire. A large snake was coiled around his shoulders. He played with it like it was a kitten or puppy.

"Wow! Would you look at that!" Lowell gasped.

The snake moved around his shoulders and neck and its tongue flicked in and out. Women in bright ankle-length skirts and silk blouses with huge cartwheel earrings went about getting the meal. Others were tending the horses.

Finally, the man turned and looked toward the road. He pulled the huge snake from his neck and held it above his head.

"What's he up to?" Mick whispered. Devil growled, his teeth bared in the sunlight.

I nudged Troop. "I think he's motioning for us to come into the camp and see the snake."

"Yeah, I think that's what he means, Carley," Troop answered.

I swallowed hard and stepped forward. Mick grabbed me by the sleeve of my shirt.

"Where you going, Bimberg? What do you think you're doing?"

I looked around. I could see fear in Mick's beady eyes. He spat nervously.

"Troop and me are going in to the camp to see what he wants."

Mick stepped back. "What? You're crazy! You walk in there and you'll never be seen again. Don't you know they kidnap kids? Ain't you got any sense at all?"

I pulled my arm away from him. "You do what you want, Mick. Troop and I are going in to see what he wants."

"You're crazy, man. That's a real dumb thing to do." He spat once again in defiance.

"I guess it is pretty scary, all right," I said. "I guess it would take some real guts to go in there and see what he wants, especially when he's holding that big snake." I started walking. Mick grabbed my shirt again.

"Wait a minute. Are you saying I'm scared, Bimberg? If that's what you're saying you'd better take it back before you find your teeth on the ground."

"I didn't say you were scared. I just said that it's pretty scary to go in there. Whether you decide to go in with us is up to you. All I can tell you is that Troop and I are going in." I motioned for Troop to follow me. Troop followed. He had no expression on his face. You could never tell by looking at him whether he was scared, sad, happy or what. He just stared straight ahead without any sort of expression.

After about ten steps, I looked back. Mick was following us. He glared at his gang, and they followed him. Devil stayed close to his master, a deep growl vibrating in him the whole time. Lowell's pink eyes were ready to pop right out of his head. Frank's face was beet red and he panted real hard.

Troop and I walked slowly into the encampment. Gypsies were everywhere. They looked up as we passed. Everything was real quiet until someone said something in a foreign language and everyone laughed. Children were playing and wrestling. They stopped and watched us walk toward the campfire. It was real cool and shady in the encampment. My nostrils twitched as I smelled a variety of things: charred wood, unwashed bodies, bubbling stew on the fire, the dampness of the weeds and foliage...everything mingled together.

We stepped up to the campfire and stared at the man caressing the snake around his neck. He had on a red turban and an earring dangled from one ear. His mustache was pencil thin beneath his large nose and his eyes were jet black. I couldn't tell if he was young or old. I guess he was in between, but his skin was very dark and looked as dry as leather.

He looked up and spoke. "You townspeople are bothering our camp. We are doing nothing wrong. We are not disturbing you. You have no right to call us names, throw rocks, or stand on the road staring at us."

I thought just then that he was right. Troop and I didn't throw rocks or call them names but we did, year after year, come and stare at them as if they were something curious.

The gypsy continued. His voice was scratchy and deep. "I do not call you brave when you do that. That is a way of a coward. You call names and throw rocks and then run scared. You should be ashamed of yourselves," he said.

Mick and his gang slowly sidled up next to us.

"We want you out of our town," Mick said boldly.

The man turned to Mick. "Why do you want this? Why are you so unkind to us?"

Mick looked over at his gang and shrugged. "We've heard all about your kind. We've heard how you put curses on people you don't like. You caused the crops to die, no rain for a month, and cows dried up last year. It happened right when you left."

"And you are saying that we gypsies caused this?" He threw his head back, laughing. "We do have powers that no one understands, but I'm afraid we are not that powerful."

"We know your kind. We know how you steal and take kids away and sell them," Mick said.

I looked down quickly at the man, expecting him to be very angry. Instead, he laughed once more.

"And then why are you here in my camp if you are so afraid that we take children and sell them? Aren't you taking a very big chance being here?"

Mick stepped back, raising his staff for protection. "You just try anything. The Sheriff will be right out here and the whole bunch of you will be in real trouble."

"You talk bravely. What is your name?"

Mick gulped, looking suspiciously around. "My name is Mick Fuller. I'm the leader of this gang."

And then if you're a leader you must be very brave. Is that not so?"

"Yeah, that's so. I ain't afraid of nothing." He puffed his chest out.

I smiled and nudged Troop, remembering Mick's long steep slide down Cave Springs Mountain a few nights ago. Troop didn't smile.

"Well, if you're not afraid of anything, you wouldn't mind passing a little test, would you?" the gypsy asked.

"What kind of test? I don't trust the likes of you," Mick said, spitting on the ground.

"It's not much of a test. It just indicates whether you are brave or not. All you have to do is allow Starlight to be friends with you."

"And who is this Starlight anyway?" Mick asked.

The man looked down at the snake he was petting.

"What are you telling me?" Mick asked.

"If you are brave, you wouldn't mind letting Starlight coil around your neck and letting my little hairy friends scamper across your bare chest and shoulders at the same time."

"What? You must think I'm crazy!" Mick screamed. He gripped his staff tighter, I noticed.

"That is a real test of bravery. Starlight or my hairy little pets will not harm a truly brave man. But, if you show fear or flinch, then..." He paused, smiling sinisterly.

A bunch of goose bumps popped out on my arms.

"It'd take a fool to let a big snake coil around his neck and a bunch of spiders crawl all over him." Mick poked his chest with his thumb. "And Mick Fuller ain't no fool. Anyone can tell you that." He looked around and his gang nodded.

"It does not take a fool to do such a thing. It takes a very brave man. If he shows no fear and is a true believer, he will not be harmed." He turned to Mick. "Are you such a person? Or are you just a person who uses his mouth instead of his bravery?"

Mick clutched his staff and Devil growled, his mane standing straight up on his neck.

"All I can tell you Mister, is that I ain't letting no snake or spiders parade all over me. No one here is that big of an idiot." He looked around confidently.

68

"I'll do it." I gulped. I couldn't believe I just said such a thing. It had to be someone else. It was like the time I had a real high fever with the measles and I said things that I didn't mean or know about. What in the world made me blurt out such a crazy thing? I asked myself in the back of my mind. Troop looked at me. This time his face did have an expression. He looked at me with his eyes wide open. I could tell he was silently asking, "What are you saying, you idiot?"

The gypsy smiled. He had the whitest teeth I've ever seen in a human mouth. They looked like rows of pearls.

"There is a brave man among us. We have a real man to demonstrate his courage and bravery."

Mick stood there, his mouth hanging wide open.

The gypsy patted a spot next to him. I walked over to him and slowly sat down. The snake weaved about his neck and turned its head to smell me. I sat there as stiff as a stick.

"Let us begin the test of courage," the gypsy said. He clapped his hands and a small, brown child ran to him, carrying a cigar box. Even though it was cool in the hollow, sweat ran off me in rivers.

"Now, young lad, remove your shirt and the test will begin."

I gulped. Slowly I unbuttoned my shirt. The rest of the gypsy tribe came closer. They crowded around, smiling, waiting for the test.

Mick jumped forward. "Wait a minute! Bimberg ain't as brave as I am. I'll take the test!"

His gang shouted and applauded.

"Move over Bimberg!" he ordered. "I'll show you how a real man acts."

Quickly, he removed his torn shirt, flinging it to the ground.

"Well, it looks like the boy with the big mouth has courage to match after all." The gypsy moved so Mick could sit next to him.

Mick sat there naked to the waist, waiting. He spat and nervously licked his upper lip.

The gypsy pulled the huge snake from his shoulders and carefully draped it around Mick's shoulders. I couldn't help but notice the bunches of goose bumps popping out all over Mick's chest. His eyes squinted shut just as tight as he could get them. The snake slithered around his neck, flicking its tongue in and out.

"Now, for the final part of the test of courage..." The gypsy took the cigar box from the young boy and opened it. There were at least twenty big hairy spiders running all over in the bottom of the box. Reaching in, the gypsy caught one and placed it on Mick's bare arm. Mick kept his eyes closed tighter than a drum. The spider hesitated and then began running all over Mick's arm. The gypsy placed a spider on Mick's shoulder and a couple on his bare chest.

Everyone was quiet. Mick shuddered. He was breathing real hard. Suddenly, he threw his eyelids open and stared down at the hairy creatures running all over him. His mouth flung open, first in a gasp of disbelief, and then opened wider, and he yelled so loud it echoed back from the hills in the distance. Jumping to his feet, he pulled the snake from his neck, flinging it down to the hard ground. His hands flew to his shoulder and chest, brushing away the spiders. He moved like lightning hollering all the while, dancing, crazy-like, in place. He ran back to the group, cussing and fuming like mad.

Everyone in the camp started laughing. It started out as sort of a snicker or two but ended up in a whole chorus of loud, teary-eyed belly laughs. Mick stood there tight-lipped, eyeing everyone.

Once the gypsy got control of himself, he looked over at me. "Now, let us try the bravery test on the first volunteer. It seems the one with the large mouth did not have the bravery to match, afterall."

My mouth went dry as I tried to swallow. The gypsy

picked up the snake and laid it around my shoulders. It felt heavy, wet and slick, and I felt its ribs pushing in and out as it slithered around my shoulders. Its little tongue hit at my face and cheek. I thought about that Osage copperhead Troop and I saw not long ago. I shivered. I looked up at Troop for support. He made a fist and shook it at me.

"Now, for the final test." The gypsy nodded and the brown boy brought the cigar box to him again. He opened the top and fished out a couple of the big, hairy spiders. I had read and heard how just one nip by some kinds of hairy scorpions could mean sudden death. Sweat rolled off my forehead. I tried to imagine I was somewhere else...anywhere. In my mind, I imagined I was laying right beneath that willow tree back home, listening to the rustling leaves and the whining mosquitoes and smelling the sweet Williams and verbena. Or maybe I was pulling a fat bullhead out of Turtle Creek, or skipping flat rocks, or even climbing Cave Springs Mountain. Anything would be better than this.

They were crawling all over me. Hundreds of tiny little legs running all over my arms, shoulders, and chest. It was all I could do to keep from screaming my head off. I looked down and shuddered. There they were scampering all over me. It looked like hundreds of them, but I know there were only about twenty. The snake moved around my neck and flicked at my ears. The spiders moved all over me, some even crawling up my chin, running right beneath my eyes. When I looked at them they looked bigger than horses.

Everyone waited. There was not a sound. I forced my eyes to stay open but I also forced my mind to be somewhere else. Otherwise, I knew I wouldn't be able to stand it. I could just hear what my Ma would say if she saw me. And here she was sure that the worst thing I was doing was drinking too many Green Rivers or tearing the tape off of Peterson's comic books.

71

After five minutes the gypsy took the spiders off me and put them back into the cigar box. He took them off slowly, one by one. After the last one was put in the box, he lifted the snake from my shoulders. I felt so weak I nearly fell over on my face.

He smiled at me.

"This boy has proved his courage. He has passed both tests. We will make him an honorary member of the Moravian Tribe. He will always be welcome in our camp!"

The cheers went up and rang in my ears. Troop ran over and lifted me to my feet, beating me on the back with congratulations. I was dizzy, partly from the scare and partly because of the great honor being put on me. Everyone in camp was hollering his head off.

Out of the corner of my eye I saw Mick, his face red with anger, motioning to the Spiders to get. They never waited when Mick looked like that. They were gone in a split second, every last one of them.

"We are all proud of you, brother," the gypsy said. "That took great courage," he said, smiling. "Of course, the snake is harmless. It is a boa constrictor and not poisonous in the least. And the spiders are not scorpions but harmless wood spiders. They are not dangerous either, but you did not know this. You passed the test feeling that you were in grave danger. That is the mark of true courage!"

Again, the tribe cheered and Troop hollered just as loud as anyone. I smiled, raising my fists. I felt about nine feet tall all of a sudden. It was the greatest feeling on earth.

When the cheering quieted down and everyone went back to his duties, the gypsy spoke. Reaching down, he grabbed my hand with the handkerchief around it. "What happened to your hand, brave lad?"

"I...I got bit this morning by my pet coon, Shiner. He clamped his teeth in me."

Slowly, the gypsy unwrapped my hand and looked at the crusted blood and the holes where Shiner's teeth had been.

"You are brave and a member of our tribe now. I will cure your hand. You will have nothing to worry about." He clapped his hands together and a boy ran to him, carrying a sack. He took the sack from the boy and opened it. Peering inside, he studied the contents for some time. At last, he pulled out a flat rock and handed it to me.

"Here is an amulet. It will cure your wound. It is the most powerful amulet we have. The fossil in the rock is in the shape of a horse's head. We worship the horse for its grace, beauty, and power. Sleep with the amulet under your pillow tonight, and when you awaken unwrap your hand and your wound will be gone. Be sure not to look at it until morning, however," he warned.

Troop looked skeptically at me. I took the rock and nodded. "Thank you. I will do just as you say. I'll put it under my pillow for the night. I believe that my wound will be gone tomorrow morning."

"You are a true believer. That will surely make the amulet work for you. You are not only brave but you are a gypsy at heart. That is good." He smiled, clapping me on the back.

He pointed toward the bridge. "Go now, and we will see you next year when we return." He smiled. "Goodbye, brother."

Troop and I shook hands with the gypsy and headed out of the camp toward the bridge. We looked back and waved several times and every member of the tribe waved back.

I sure changed my feelings about gypsies after that day. And to think I was an honorary member of the Moravian Tribe. That was really special. I understood them better now. They weren't all those bad things people said. And I especially believed in them when I woke up the next morning and unwrapped my hand, finding it a whole lot better. It made me wonder if the gypsies really did possess magic.

Chapter 7

The summer went on. It was one of those hot, lazy summers where your feet practically stuck to the road. Not much happened for the next couple weeks, except Pa let me keep Shiner with the understanding that I'd take care of him and that he would tame down and not be dangerous. Neither Pa nor Ma knew Shiner had bit me, and of course, with the gypsy giving me the amulet and it helping the wound disappear, they'd never know. Well, maybe I'd tell them someday, like when I got old and had my own family and they'd be grandparents. That way, I'd be too old to have Pa take the strap to me. Of course, he never really did that very often, anyhow. Pa was pretty nice most of the time. He even brought Shiner things to eat from the store. Scraps of fish, carrots, broken cookies, — that animal would eat anything, that's for sure. Shiner's foot did mend, and he let me pick him up, pet him, everything. He usually perched on my shoulder, watching all the comings and goings of everyone. He was the most curious critter I ever saw. All the kids in town were envious of Shiner. He was the neatest pet around. Much better than an old dog. I felt real proud to have him. The thing was, other than me, Troop, Ma and Pa, Shiner didn't trust anyone else.

The candle flickered on the wooden crate and tallow ran down the sides in thick drips. Funny large shadows hovered about the walls. The damp, cold ground came up through the old blanket I laid down to sit on. Shiner raised up on his hind legs sniffing around. It was scary to me, but I wasn't about to say anything, that's for sure. All the Mustangs sat huddled together, staring at the candle on the crate. The meetings always were better at night in that shed we called our club house by the creek. The wind whistled outside, and shadows flitted across the walls from the trees buffeting back and forth. The horse skull fastened to the wall hovered over us. It was real neat-looking on the wall. We took it down after the meeting and buried it safely away so no one would find it, and then we'd hang it up next meeting. Lizards scurried around in a cardboard box making little scratchy noises with their feet. They were our mascots.

Darrell Salsburg's eyes were as big as Ma's new saucers. This was his big night; he was being officially initiated into the Mustangs. Initiations were always at night. Everyone but Pee Wee Carter got out to come to the meeting. Pee Wee, red-faced and teary-eyed, explained that there was no way his Ma was going to let him out to run the streets after eight o'clock. He said he'd begged until he turned green, but had no luck.

So, all the rest of the members sat Indian-fashioned around the crate waiting for Troop to speak. Troop was the initiation chairman. Troop waited for several moments to build up the suspense. He was great at that. Shiner nervously paced around on my shoulder. I think he felt like he'd like something to start happening. Troop raised the cow bone we used as a gavel to bring our meeting to order. Every eye turned to him. "The initiation will be tonight!" He said it all dramatic-like, though of course we knew the initiation would be tonight. That's why we were all there. That's why everyone tried so hard to get out of the house after dark. But, I guess Troop was just saying it that way to have a scary effect because I saw Darrell's adam's apple jump like crazy.

"We have thought a long time on what the initiation will be. We've all been through the initiation into the Mustangs. This initiation proves your worthiness to be a Mustang. It shows bravery and boldness. We've had some who had to spend all night in Radcliffe's haunted house. Some had to ride a goat down main street. Some had to stay two hours out at Mount Hope Cemetery during a full moon. But tonight we have something special for Brother Darrell...."

All heads turned to Darrell. His head sank down into his shoulders. Everyone waited for Troop to finish.

"It is an honor to be a Mustang. You don't get to be a Mustang just because you want to. You have to be chosen and then you have to prove yourself to be a Mustang."

Troop sure knew how to say the right things, I thought. He was really impressing Darrell and the rest of the members. I could hardly wait to see what he had cooked up for him tonight.

"Stand and face the Council, Brother Darrell!" Troop ordered.

Darrell gulped, getting to his feet. His shadow loomed on the wall. His hands were clenched tight.

Troop raised the cow bone once again, letting it drop on the crate with a bang. "Your initiation will be to travel out to Luke Webster's farm and swim in his pond."

Darrell looked around for help. He thought that there had been a mistake. Luke Webster had been out of jail only a week. No one in his right mind would set foot on his property. There were signs all over stating that any trespasser would be shot on sight. Only weeks ago, Luke had gone berserk up town, shooting windows out and scaring the daylights out of everyone.

No one offered Darrell any help. Everyone was very glad that he wasn't the one who had to do such a dangerous thing.

"Tonight?" Darrell squeaked.

"Yes, tonight," demanded Troop. And then his eyes squinted. "You're not scared to do it, are you? You're not telling the Mustangs that you're not man enough to go out to Luke Webster's and swim in his pond, are you?"

Everybody was silent. I couldn't help feeling a little

sorry for Darrell. He shifted from one foot to the other like he suddenly had to go to the bathroom. He probably did.

Darrell shook his head. "I ain't saying that. I'm just saying that maybe my ma and pa would be real mad if I went clear out there, especially in the dark. Everyone knows that he's plum crazy. There's no telling what he'd do to a body if he caught him out there on his property."

"Then you're saying that you refuse to go through the initiation? Is that correct?" Troop asked him. Troop's voice was deep and strong. I could see that Darrell was wilting.

"I...I ain't saying... I...all right, I'll do it." He shrugged his shoulders in defeat.

Larry McKracken raised his hand and was recognized. "How're we going to be sure that Brother Darrell goes clear out to Luke Webster's and swims in his pond? For all we would know Darrell may head out that way but slip in a ditch or hide behind some trees or whatever and just wait a long time. And then he might jump into some farmer's cow tank and come back dripping and all of us might think that he really did go out to Luke Webster's." He looked proudly around. He was proud for finding the loopholes in the plan.

"That's a good point," Troop said. He thought for a moment. "I know. We'll have to have proof. Two of us will have to go along with him to be sure he carries it out, that's all." He looked around. "I need two volunteers to go along with Brother Darrell to be sure the initiation is carried out the way it should be."

It got as quiet as a graveyard. All the members either looked down or pretended to be very interested in the horse skull on the wall.

Troop's jaw became set. "Well, in that case I guess I'll have to go with Brother Darrell. And I think our president should go along with us as well."

I looked up, taken off guard.

"Don't you think that would be fair, President Carley?" Troop asked.

Well, what could I say? I couldn't ask any member of the club to do something I wouldn't do. It wouldn't be fair, and besides they'd lose faith in me as their leader. I had only one thing to do.

I cleared my throat. "You're right, Brother Troop. You and I will go with Brother Darrell to see that he carries out the initiation the way it should be carried out. After all, we are the leaders of this club. It would be right for us to go along."

Fats and Henry started clapping and everyone followed. There wasn't much Troop and I could do but go along with Darrell out to Luke Webster's farm.

The moon was a big bright pumpkin hanging in the sky, giving us plenty of light so we could see the ruts and rocks in the road. It lit up the humps of the Flint Hills in the distance. It was a warm breezy night. We walked a while, ran a while, and paused once in a while to throw some rocks or count fence posts. Darrell kind of forgot what the whole thing was about on the way. The whole thing didn't seem all that scary with three of us out there, playing games and all. We told some ghost stories just to make it a little more scary. Everything was pretty light until we came to the place where we turned off to Luke Webster's pasture. We got real quiet as though Luke was just behind us or something.

"Here's where we turn in, Brothers," I said.

Through the darkness, we saw the signs posted with the usual skull and crossbones as a warning.

"I...I don't suppose there's anything to worry about. Actually, Luke lives way down the road. He's probably in bed, or listening to the radio or something. We'll be here and gone and he'll never know about it," Darrell said, trying to act brave.

Troop clapped him on the shoulder. "That's the spirit, Brother Darrell. That shows real courage. And you're right. We'll be here and gone and he'll never know about it. You're right there."

"Well, what we waiting for anyway?" Darrell cried. "Let's get in there and take us a swim. I'm mighty hot walking these five miles."

We crawled through the barbed wire fence. While I pushed my way through the skeins of fence, Troop held Shiner for me, but then Shiner bounced right back up on my shoulder. He stood on two legs, while we ran down the steep incline toward the pond, nestled neatly in the middle of Luke's pasture. Shucking out of our clothes, we ran bare as new born babies to the water, whooping and hollering and having a heck of a time.

Shiner stayed on the bank, running back and forth and seeming to be having just as much fun as we were. The mud squished between my toes as my feet sank into it. When I got out deeper, I fell head first into the pond. It was warm as bath water and felt real good. I lay back and floated for a time. Heck, I thought, this initiation wasn't anything at all. Brother Darrell was lucky Troop thought of this one for him.

Troop came up from behind me, pushing me under. I yelled, coming up spitting and blowing water everywhere. And then all of us had a grand water fight. It's a wonder we all didn't drown. But, boy, was it fun! Out of breath, I found a log floating along the bank. I thought it would be fun to have Shiner join us out there in the middle of the pond. I put him on it and pulled the log on out, with him scampering around on top of it. He stood on his hind legs, running back and forth. I knew I was one lucky kid to have such a great pet as Shiner.

We floated him around the pond for about an hour, yelling and pretending that we were a shipwrecked crew hanging on to a life raft. It was more fun than a barrel of monkeys.

Suddenly, we looked over at Troop and stopped everything. Nobody's got ears like Troop and he was standing there, still as a stick, looking toward the grove of trees next to the pond.

"What's the matter, Troop?" I asked.

Troop said nothing. He put his finger to his lips telling me to be quiet.

Brother Darrell stopped splashing and got real still.

Troop started to slowly walk toward us.

"Something wrong?" I asked.

"There's something out there," Troop said in a whisper.

"What do you mean there's something out there?" I know that was a stupid question.

"Something or someone is watching us from over there in the trees," Troop replied.

"How can you tell?" I asked. "It's dark as pitch over there." I should've known better. He has a sense about such things. He just knows when something isn't right. I should've believed him right away.

"Maybe it's just some cattle or something. After all, this is a cattle pond," Darrell offered hopefully.

Troop shook his head. "No, it's not cattle. It's not that many."

"Maybe it's just one cow, then," I said.

Troop shook his head again. "I can't tell how many, but it's watching us from somewhere over there." He pointed to a thick grove of trees.

Goose bumps popped out all over my flesh. I squinted, trying to see in the dark. Naturally, I couldn't see a thing.

"Maybe we'd better get," Darrell said, his teeth shaking.

I looked over at Shiner nervously prancing back and forth on the log. I think he sensed that there was something over there too. "Our clothes are clear out of reach over there," I said biting into my lip.

"Look!" Troop said. "I saw someone move over there in those bushes."

All three of us started shaking. We folded our arms around ourselves. Even though it was summer and the water was warm, we suddenly got chills down our spines.

I looked to where Troop was pointing and saw something move through the bushes. Shivers trailed down my back. I should've known Troop couldn't be wrong. Quickly, I picked up Shiner and put him on my shoulder. I thought if we'd have to escape fast I didn't want to leave him behind. I wouldn't do that on a bet.

"Listen to me," Troop said. "Let's walk real slow to the bank. Once we get there, let's run as fast as we can, grab our clothes, and high-tail it out of here. That's about all we can do."

"Y...y...yes, I guess you're right," Darrell stammered.

We took a step and then another toward the bank. My heart beat so loud I thought the other two could hear it. At that moment, I would've given my monarch collection, my new ball glove, and my bag of prize marbles to be home in bed.

The bushes parted and a huge figure moved out of them. The moon settled on the figure, making it look all that much more scary. He stood there straight as string on a big horse just staring at us. We backed into the water gasping, our mouths wide open.

"It's Luke!" I cried. "He heard us and we're dead sure!"

We stood in the water, waiting for him to raise his shotgun and mow us down one by one. I knew this was it. They'd find all three of us floating face down in the pond in the morning. I repeated a little prayer Ma taught me as a little kid. I supposed he'd legally be set free since we had no business there in the first place. I stroked Shiner. It made me feel a little better.

Darrell clutched my arm so tight I just about hollered. "I'm sorry I ever wanted to get into your darned club," he said under his breath. He was shaking like a leaf.

My flesh crawled as the huge buckskin galloped down

toward the pond. Luke screeched that high-pitched woman's sound. It was so eerie it about made me sick. He kept screaming and galloping toward us with his shotgun raised over his head. None of us said a word. We didn't even breathe. We stood there naked as jaybirds, the water only up to our knees, awaiting our fate.

The ground thundered and shook as the big horse galloped closer and closer. All three of us knew we were goners for sure. Luke screeched in a high-pitched wavering sound and thundered right up to the bank of the pond. Swooping down, he snatched up our pile of clothes and before you could say "Jack Robinson," he galloped back into the trees and was gone.

"Where...where'd he go?" I asked.

"Who cares as long as he's gone," Darrell said, through chattering teeth.

"We'd better get out of here right away before he takes a notion to come back," Troop wisely stated.

All three of us ran out of the water, hopping and skipping whenever our feet hit a sharp rock. But we didn't take all that much of a notice. At the moment we just wanted to get out of there alive. A few bruised feet was the least of our worries.

It wasn't until we scaled the fence and were back on the road, panting like fat dogs, did we realize that here we were five miles from home, late at night, and naked as jaybirds!

We heard the big buckskin's heavy hooves clopping up the hill out of sight. Every now and then Luke screamed real shrill, and goose bumps popped out all over us from the bottom of our feet to the top of our scalps. And being the way we were, we had plenty of room for goose bumps.

"This is some initiation," Darrell said bitterly, all scrunched up to cover all the embarrassing parts with his hands. "How in the heck are we going to get out of this mess without someone seeing us?"

Shiner scampered back and forth. He knew something was wrong. I leaned down, picked him up, and put him on my bare shoulder. I felt his little claws pinch at my skin. He stood up on his hind legs making little chirping sounds.

"Would we know something like this would happen, for gosh sakes? You can't tell what old Luke will do. He's got a lot of empty space in his attic," I said, trying to be funny.

Troop placed his hands on his hips, studying the situation. It was a hot night, but being the way we were made us start to get chilled.

I rubbed my bare arms.

"Well, we could break off some branches and hold them in front and back of us. That would cover us a little, wouldn't it?" Troop asked with a funny sound in his voice.

"Yeah, but what about when we get into town? Those street lights are gonna light us up like all get out. And how are we gonna explain all this to our folks?" I said, shuddering.

"I'll get a trip to the woodshed sure as the world," Darrell said solemnly. "I'll never be able to explain this."

"Well," I said, clearing my throat, "we can stand out here all night jawing until the sun comes up, or we can get back to town and take our medicine like men. If we wait until the sun comes up we're going to be in real trouble."

"Carley's right," Troop said. "Let's get some branches and head back to town. We're not getting anything done here."

"Right!" we all said and started breaking off branches as fast as we could.

I've got to admit it was a funny sight; us three guys going tippy-toe down the road as naked as the day we came into the world. But at the time, it sure didn't seem funny to us. At least none of us were laughing. I'm sure each of us was thinking hard of what he was going to say to explain what he was doing way out at Luke Webster's land skinny dipping in his pond late at night. It was going to take some tall explaining, that's for sure.

We walked about three miles, trying our best to stay in the shadows because that old moon lit up our white skin like you wouldn't believe.

"Look!" shouted Troop.

"What?" I jumped back behind a tree, sure he spotted someone coming.

"There's some clothes over there flapping on that clothesline." He pointed in the distance.

I squinted. Sure as the world those eyes of his didn't fail him. A farmer's wife left her clothes out on the line over night and there they were, flapping in the wind like they were alive.

"We could sneak in there and get some, just enough to cover us to get into town. We could bring them back to her sometime later," Darrell said, nodding eagerly.

I stood there thinking over the situation. We sure were in a pickle. Finally, I nodded. "Okay, but we'd better be careful because whenever there's a farm there's a farm dog and most of them have teeth a mile long."

Shiner chattered excitedly on my shoulder.

"Let's quit talking and get going. I'm cold," Darrell whined.

"Okay, let's do it," I said and ran toward the gate.

Once there, we stopped and looked right, and then left, and then all around for signs of life, especially a big dog.

Troop nodded his okay. If he couldn't see anything, there wasn't anything there. Carefully, I unlatched the gate. The squeal of the hinges made my teeth grind together. It sounded louder than a six-inch firecracker on the Fourth. We looked around and then scampered through the gate toward the clothesline.

With a swipe, I pulled a pair of overalls off the line. It felt good to be covered again. Troop pulled another pair off and slipped them on, hauling the bib straps over his shoulders and rolling the cuffs.

"Hey, wait a minute!" Darrell screamed.

Troop and I jumped out of our skins.

"What you trying to do," I whispered, "wake the dead? Gee, be quiet. We've been real lucky so far."

"Sure, that's fine for you to say," argued Darrell. "I wouldn't call it all that lucky with just that left on the line." Darrell pointed to the remaining clothing.

All that was left was some filmy curtains and a full length lady's apron flapping in the wind. I looked at Troop and saw his white teeth grinning in the dark.

Darrell put his hands on his hips. "What am I going to do? You guys got pants, but look what I've got to pick from."

The front porch screen swung open. We fell to the ground as a silhouette of a big man pranced around on the porch, sniffing the air as though he was sure something wasn't what it should be.

I patted Shiner so he'd calm down. None of us breathed. I saw the cold outline of a big old double barrel shotgun laying in his arm. Sweat rolled off my forehead. He looked all around the yard ready to aim that gun at anything that moved. Shiner crept down beside me, poking his head beneath my arm. I suppose he remembered hunters and that memory wasn't all that good to him.

All three of us lay as flat as we could on the ground. I took a breath as the big farmer shrugged his shoulders and walked back into the house. I thanked the Lord that I'd be able to live to see Christmas.

"Now, quit your whining," Troop whispered to Darrell, "and get something from the clothesline so we can get out of here."

"Ahhh," Darrell moaned, "this is downright humiliating."

He pulled the lady's flowered apron from the line and tied it tightly around his waist. It came down to his ankles. The only thing wrong was that his backside was completely exposed and shined white as a sheet in the night. If the situation wasn't so serious, me and Troop would've rolled on the ground with gut-busting laughter. But, it wasn't time for laughter. It was time for getting back on the road and high-tailing it out of there.

Darrell tugged on the apron trying to get it to cover as much skin as possible, but it was a long way from reaching all the way around.

At last, the three of us started tippy-toeing back toward the gate. We hadn't taken five steps when the biggest, meanest looking farm dog came bounding out from beneath the porch. The hair stood straight up on his neck and his bark echoed back from the flint hills in the distance. Troop, Darrell, and I screamed with surprise and fear and straight up ordered our feet to start flying. Troop made it to the gate first, but I wasn't far behind. We didn't take time to open the gate but hurtled right over it, racing down the dirt road. Suddenly, we wondered what had happened to Darrell. Both of us looked back and nearly swallowed our adam's apples. There was poor old Darrell, screeching like a trapped polecat, pulling at the bottom of that apron which was clamped like a vice in the jaws of that farm dog.

Troop and I stood there dumbfounded, not knowing which way to go. Darrell pulled this way and that, trying to pull that apron loose and screeching the whole time. That big dog held tight, pulling and growling like all get out. I looked at Troop and Troop looked at me and we both shrugged not knowing what to do. After all, Darrell was a Brother Mustang now, beings he had been duly initiated and all. We just about decided to jump back over the fence and give old Darrell a hand when that big farmer stepped back out on the porch and aimed his shotgun plum at Darrell.

Troop and I fell face first to the ground, expecting buckshot to start whizzing over our heads. We lay there, our noses pressed in the dust, on the road. A blast of a shotgun shook the earth and Darrell screamed so loud his tonsils nearly flew out of his mouth.

We raised our heads just in time to see Brother Darrell catapult the gate like a thoroughbred jumper at the State Fair and tear toward us down the road. Another shot blasted and Darrell screamed again. We looked up just in time to see a big hole torn in the front of Darrell's apron from the dog. But that was nothing as he raced past without once looking at us laying there. His whole backside lit in the moonlight racing toward town.

Troop looked at me, trying to hold back a grin. "Well, Carley," he said, "I suppose Brother Darrell will quit the Mustangs for sure, and right after his initiation, too."

Chapter 8

The ripe wheat waved in the fields and seemed to go on endlessly. It was one of those lazy old summer days. The kind of day when you just don't want to do a thing except breathe or sip on a cold lemonade or dabble your toes in a creek or something.

Today, I was all by myself. I had finished my chores and was considering joining the rest of the guys playing baseball near the school. For some reason though, I couldn't muster up enough energy to play baseball. All I wanted to do was lay on the bank of Turtle Creek and dip my toes in the water and maybe watch Shiner scamper around, chasing grasshoppers. I didn't have one bit of energy. I had my pole in the water so at least somebody wouldn't think I was crazy laying here like this. I didn't even know if it was baited. I really didn't care. I had a pretty good bite a little while ago, but I just didn't have the gumption to check it out, so the bullhead probably already had all my bait.

Smiling to myself, I watched Shiner jump up and down, trying to catch those grasshoppers in mid air. He sure was having a good time. I couldn't get over how good he looked now in just over a month. He'd fattened out and was good as new. I was sure glad I had him as a pet. It was times like this that I was particularly glad because he was all the company I needed.

I giggled as Shiner went head over heels in the grass. Yep, he was really having himself a time, I thought, stretching myself out on the cool bank. I tipped my straw hat over my eyes so I could take a little snooze.

A rock as big as my head suddenly exploded in the creek, splashing water all over me. I threw my hat back and jumped to my feet, wiping my face with the back of my hand and scowling when I saw who'd thrown the rock. I should've known. There was Mick Fuller, standing at the top of the bank, just as big as you please, smiling like a cat who caught a canary. Frank and Lowell were right with him, as usual, and of course, Devil. Mick laughed and laughed.

"That surprised you, didn't it, Bimberg?" he said, grinning. "Probably thought there wasn't a soul around for miles."

Frank and Lowell joined him, laughing their heads off.

My jaw tightened, as it always did when Mick was around. "I had a darned good bite, Mick. If you caused me to lose it..." I paused, trying to think of something. In truth, that bite went away over fifteen minutes ago.

"You'll what, Bimberg? You'd better watch how you threaten. You might have to carry it out," Mick warned.

"Ah, why don't you and your gang get lost, Mick? Can't you leave a guy in peace?" I asked.

"I don't have to if I don't want to, Bimberg. This creek ain't your property. So quit acting like you own it."

"You're right, there," I agreed. "But, I'm fishing here. There's plenty of the creek and miles of bank left if you and your gang want to fish."

Mick pushed his hat back with his thumb. With his staff in his hand, he started down the bank toward me, Devil right next to him. Frank and Lowell followed at a respectful distance.

Mick stopped a few feet in front of me, glaring with those beady grey eyes. He pointed his staff at Shiner, who froze in the grass, making some pretty scary sounds. Devil growled, soft-like, in reply, but didn't leave Mick's side. "You and that mangy coon having a good time clear out here?" he asked with a sneer. "I wouldn't be seen dead with a pet like that. He looks like he's been chewed up by a pack of hounds."

My face got red hot. I didn't like him or anybody talking that way about Shiner. "He's just as good as your old dog, Mick," I said nodding toward Devil.

Devil's lion mane stood up and his upper lip pulled back; he nearly roared. He knew that I just said something bad about him. I backed up a little bit.

"Better watch yourself or Devil will chew your leg off," Mick warned. "He don't like many people and you're on the list of people he really don't like."

"So?" I said. I couldn't think of anything else to say.

Frank laughed and Lowell swiped his snow white hair back from his forehead.

"We never did discuss you making a fool out of me with those gypsies a few weeks back," Mick said, his face getting blood red. "I'm still real hot about that. I don't like being made a fool of, I can tell you that. I'm more man than you'll ever be."

"Sure you are, Mick," I said, grinning.

Bolting forward in one leap, Mick grabbed the bib of my overalls. "I've about had all I can take from you this summer. Every time we meet, you make me mad...real mad. And I ain't going to stand for it! Today, we're going to have a showdown."

That was some more of his cowboy western talk. My stomach tightened. "I suppose you'd be willing to do that, especially when I'm outnumbered three to one." I tried to sound brave.

"I'll tell Frank and Lowell to stay out of it. It'd be just between me and you, Bimberg."

I found myself thinking I sure wished Troop was here. He was always a good one to depend on in a fight. He was always at my side. I shook my head. "I don't want to fight you, Mick. All I want to do is lay here, fish, and mind my own business. I'm not hurting you or anyone else."

"Yeah, but you did hurt me a few weeks ago with those gypsies. I've never forgotten that. And the more I think about it, the madder I get. I'm not going to be satisfied until your eyes are black as that coon's and your nose is bleeding good and proper."

Frank and Lowell giggled, enjoying Mick's smooth words. Mick threw his staff down and tossed his hat to the ground. When he did that, he was really getting ready for a fight. I sighed and threw my hat off as well. I thought I might as well get it over with because we would never be done with it until Mick had his revenge.

Shiner, sensing something was wrong, hurried toward me. He stopped, standing on his hind legs, pawing the air toward Mick and Devil. My heart warmed seeing that. That was some great pet, I thought.

"That critter better watch himself or he's in for it. All I've got to do is sic Devil on him and he's had it."

I bit my lower lip. As much as I hated to admit it, Mick was right. I'd seen Devil hurt dogs and cats real bad in the past. I sure didn't want Shiner to get hurt.

"Stay back, Shiner," I warned. "It's all right. Don't worry. I can handle it."

But that spunky little guy just kept right on coming, pawing the air at Devil.

Mick looked back at Frank and Lowell. I knew he was impressed, but he wasn't going to admit it. And he was making darned sure that Frank and Lowell weren't either.

Mick turned back around, his eyes little slits. He looked as mean as his dog. "I've warned that mangy little critter and now I'm getting tired of it." He looked down at Devil, and Devil met his eyes as though he was waiting for that all important command. "Sic 'em, Devil! Take care of him!" he hollered.

Before I could reach out and snatch Shiner to safety, Devil lunged forward. Frank and Lowell hurried down the rest of the way of the bank. They wanted to watch the battle.

Before you knew it, Devil was on Shiner and had him by the scruff of his neck, throwing him back and forth like a rag doll. Shiner's teeth were bared and he kept swiping the air, trying to hit Devil's nose.

"Pull him off!" I yelled. "Pull him off!"

Mick was laughing so hard he was doubled up.

Shiner squealed painfully. I rushed forward, not caring whether I got bit or not. I knew I had to save Shiner and fast. Just as I got there Devil reared back, taking Shiner with him.

Shiner managed to wiggle free, his fur all ruffled and missing in some spots. He crouched back on his hind legs and pawed the air, daring Devil to come close. He looked like a little hairy boxer.

Devil lunged again and again, trying to set his sharp fangs in Shiner. He jumped back with a sharp yip as Shiner's sharp claws caught him on the nose. A dribble of blood leaked out of his nose. He stood back, looking quizzically at Shiner, trying to figure out how he did that.

Mick stopped laughing and spat angrily on the ground.

"If that critter hurt my dog you're in for it, Bimberg," he warned.

I jumped straight up, yelling for Shiner to keep up the good work. But, it was all too good to be true. The big red chow knocked Shiner off his feet and had him down. I saw Shiner struggling to get back up, but Devil had him down on his back and he was trying to be sure he kept him down. I jumped forward, yanking Devil's curled tail as straight as a string. Devil turned around, growling at me, allowing Shiner just enough time to weakly get to his feet and scramble away. Devil wheeled back to Shiner in pursuit. Shiner ran to the nearest tree and scrambled to the top branch. He ran back and forth on the upper branch, chattering as Devil barked angrily at him from below.

"Hey, Bimberg, you pulled my dog's tail. That's not fair!"

Mick spat and hurled himself in front of me, staring down at me nose to nose.

"What do you mean, not fair?" I asked. "Devil is ten times bigger and weighs ten times more than Shiner. He would've killed him if I hadn't done something. And I'm not about to let that happen."

"That fight was just between the two of them. You keep your mits off him. When he comes down, Devil will get him good!" He looked back at Frank and Lowell with an evil grin on his face.

"In that case, I'll keep Shiner up there all day if I have to. Your dog is known to tear animals apart. There's no telling what he'd do to Shiner."

Mick giggled. "He's just like his master, a chicken...a real chicken. It's any wonder you don't crow."

Lowell laughed in a high-pitched voice.

"Don't say that about me or my pet, Mick," I warned.

"Yeah, and what you going to do if I do say that, Bimberg?"

Mick shoved my chest, and I fell on the ground. I was really hot mad. Sometimes, when I really get mad, my head starts to itch and this time it was about to drive me crazy. Slowly, my eyes narrowed as I got to my feet. I made a dive for Mick's legs, knocking him to the ground. Mick let out a grunt when his back hit the hard bank. I was on top of him swinging for all I'm worth. Devil was growling but I was so busy with Mick, I barely heard him. I fell backward when Mick hit me square in the eye. A knot started forming right away. Before I could get him back, he was on top of me, driving me to the ground. His punches hit me in the face from every direction. Devil grabbed hold of my pants leg. He growled, bit, and pulled. It was like having huge jaws pull at me from every direction. Every time I started pushing Mick back, Devil was there pulling on my leg. I knew I was in for a bad time.

Suddenly, Devil yelped real loud, rearing back. Looking up, I saw Shiner riding his back. He'd leaped right out of the tree. He dug his claws into Devil's shoulders and clamped his needle sharp teeth onto Devil's ears. Devil swung around and around to get Shiner off, but my faithful buddy rode him like a cowboy rides a bucking horse.

Mick rolled off me, watching what was happening to his dog. Devil raced one way and then another, his head tossing in all directions as he tried to reach Shiner, but the little guy always managed to stay just inches away from the menacing jaws.

"Hey, you get that critter off my dog's back. He's biting and scratching him all up!" Mick yelled.

I laid there on the ground, smiling, cheering Shiner on. Both Frank and Lowell were quiet, watching this strange battle. Devil ran a few yards then rolled over and over, trying to throw Shiner off, but when he got back to his feet, there was Shiner, still holding on to him, his claws digging into his shoulders and his teeth clamped on his ears.

Devil ran toward the creek and jumped in, hoping to get rid of Shiner that way. But what Devil didn't plan on was that Shiner was more used to water than he ever was. Shiner floated out with him, still on top. Shiner waited until Devil got out to where it was real deep, and then he scampered up on Devil's head and ducked him soundly beneath the water.

Mick looked over at me, his little grey eyes blazing with hate. We waited a long time. Shiner was still there, as big as you please, on Devil's head. Bubbles came up from Devil and Mick started to panic.

"Hey, he's trying to drown my dog! Get him off Devil right now." He shook his fist.

I couldn't believe the fight that little fellow was putting up. He stood there proud, like a captain on the deck of his ship or something. Mick picked up some rocks and hurled them at Shiner, but he dodged them expertly. "Get him off, Bimberg!

Get him off, right now!" Mick yelled.

If it had been any other dog than Devil, and if Devil's

master had been any other person than Mick, I would've felt sorry, I suppose. But, I remembered back to the many dogs Devil hurt and him always growling and showing his teeth to everyone. Maybe he was getting what he deserved at last.

Devil was still under water. All that was showing was the tips of his ears, and Shiner had them tightly in his teeth. More bubbles came up to the surface of the creek. Mick rushed over to me. He had tears in his eyes. I couldn't believe it. I had never seen Mick Fuller cry or even seen him sorry about anything. I did know that the one thing he really cared about was his dog, Devil.

"Come on, Bimberg, call that critter off. He's going to drown Devil. He's been under for a heck of a long time. Call him off..."

I looked toward the creek, watching Shiner hold Devil under, and then I turned to Mick. His eyes were actually begging me. It was hard to believe.

"All right, I'll call him off. I'll let him let Devil up. Even though that dog of yours doesn't deserve it." I clapped my hands. "Shiner! That's enough! Let him up. He's learned his lesson. Let Devil up. Right now!"

That perky little animal raised his head toward me as if he understood every word. He stood on his hind legs on Devil's head for a few moments, and then dived head first into the creek, making his way back to the bank. Right away, Devil came up. He turned toward the bank and swam toward it. Shiner was a darned good swimmer and he got to shore way before Devil. He came right to me, scampering up onto my shoulder. The water ran off him, soaking my shirt.

Mick ran down and dragged Devil onto the bank. For a few moments, the dog laid there panting as if he'd been in a fight with a lion. He was whining like a little pup and he looked thoroughly beat. His red mane was drenched and matted.

Mick turned his head toward me shaking his fist. "You're going to get it, Bimberg. That's something else I've got to get you for. That critter of yours nearly drowned my dog. I'll get him and you for this."

Frank and Lowell were silent. They looked sheepishly at each other. I think they both felt a little foolish.

Shiner stood up, chattering, telling both Mick and Devil to just try anything; if they did, he would be ready.

Mick let Devil rest a few moments and then boosted him up the bank. Once at the top, he plopped his straw hat on his head, picked up his staff, and motioned for Frank and Lowell to follow him. He walked a few paces and then looked down the bank at Shiner and me, standing there just as big as you please.

"You haven't heard the last of this, Bimberg. Your problems are just starting. Anybody who gives me or my dog a hard time is in for it. You'd just better watch yourself, that's all," he warned.

I nodded, grinning. "Yeah, yeah, Shiner and I are real scared, Mick. Real scared," I replied confidently.

Mick shrugged and walked away. Devil, Frank, and Lowell followed him.

Once I was sure they were out of sight and out of hearing range, I lifted Shiner high into the air. "Yiiipeee!" I shouted. "That was really something. Wait 'til I tell Troop. He'll never believe it." I looked up. "Shiner, old buddy, you're a real hero!"

And believe me, he sure was that day!

Chapter 9

Pa poked a piece of homemade apple pie into his mouth followed by a big gulp of coffee. He leaned back in his chair, patting his stomach. That was the only place he was fat. Other than his stomach, he looked like a scarecrow, all arms and legs.

"Clary, you make the best pie in all of Riley County. I'm as full as a tick!"

"Thank you, Daniel. Those are the harvest apples that you couldn't sell no matter how you discounted them. They had a few tender spots on them, but they made up into some real nice pies."

"They did at that. If I wasn't ready to bust at the seams, I'd have another piece." Pulling his pipe out of his shirt pocket, he tapped it on the bottom of his shoe.

I always liked watching him get his pipe ready. It was always the same thing. Tapping it on the bottom of his shoe (a few shreds of tobacco falling to the floor), slowly opening up the draw strings of the little tobacco pouch in his back pocket, dipping the pipe in and tamping the bowl with his finger until he was satisfied that it was right firm. He'd strike a wooden match beneath the table and hold it to the bowl and puff and puff until it glowed like an autumn sunset. Then he'd hold the flaming match in front of me, and I'd blow it out and he'd smile. It was always the same. I'd breathe in the sweet smoke. It wasn't just the smoke I liked. It was the smell of my Pa and it made me feel good inside.

"Craziest things been happening," he said, drawing on the stem once more.

Ma looked up from stacking the dishes. She already had a heaping mound of suds in the sink. She'd never think to sit and talk a spell after supper. No, right after we ate, it was time to get those dishes done and put away. That's the way she always was. She always said: A stitch in time...something like that.

"Yep," Pa continued, not waiting for a response. "It's happened now four or five times." He scratched his head. "Darndest thing I ever saw."

Shiner stood up on my shoulder, nibbling a small piece of meat. He held it in his tiny paws, eating real daintily.

"Well?" Ma said. "Are you going to tell us or not? You're keeping both Carley and me in suspense."

Pa sat forward in his chair, his elbows on the table. Ma allowed that now that supper was over. She would've said something if we were still eating.

"Oh, sorry, Clary. I was just mulling it over in my mind. I'm surprised you hadn't heard about it. Belford, being such a small town and all and news traveling like wild fire."

Ma and I stopped dead still, waiting for the explanation.

"You know 'Tildy Jorgenson, don't you, Clary?"

"You mean Matilda Jorgenson, once married to Albert Jorgenson? The poor old widow who lives four or five miles east of town on the back roads?"

Pa nodded, puffing his pipe. "That's the one. Poor as a church mouse. The bank was supposed to foreclose on her next month. She's way behind in her mortgage payments."

Drying her hands on her apron, Ma sat down, deciding this story was going to take some time. Nothing could hurry Pa along when he was telling a good story.

Shiner put his wet nose in my ear and I giggled.

"That's just terrible," said Ma. "That poor old soul has lived out there practically all her life." She sighed. "I wish there was something we could do. I know we have barely enough for ourselves and you've got so many who owe you. But, I sure wish we could do something."

Pa looked up, shaking his head. "You didn't let me finish, Clary. Somebody or something is already doing something for poor old Tildy."

"What do you mean, Pa?" I asked, reaching up and nudging Shiner's nose away from my ear.

"Yes, what do you mean?" Ma asked.

"Well, seems like there's been four small miracles happening out there on Tildy's farm."

"Miracles?" I asked. "What kind of miracles?" Pa had my interest for sure now.

"Well, Tildy's been finding money to pay her mortgage payment right on the day before it's due. There's a sack of silver dollars left in the darndest places. Once in the chicken coop. Tildy heard the hens squawking and thought it was a coyote. She grabbed her rifle and went out. There in a nest set a bag of coins just as big as you please. Another time the sack was left by the pump and another time right on her front porch steps." He looked around with a puzzled expression on his face. "Now ain't that the strangest thing?"

Ma looked up to the ceiling. "Maybe the Lord is answering Tildy's call. He works in mysterious ways."

Ma was a real believing person. Without thinking, I looked up too. I don't know what I was expecting, but it seemed like the thing to do.

Pa cleared his throat and we both lowered our heads. "One time she found a sack in the hay loft." He shook his head. "It sure is strange," he repeated.

"And when does this happen?" Ma asked.

"Always before the day the payment's due. The last day of the month, beings the payment is due on the first."

"That's harder yet to understand," I said, beneath my breath.

Ma's face was red. "Well, I don't think so. Don't you think the Lord would know when Tildy's payment is due? Of course, He would. He knows everything, doesn't He?

He knows every thought and every movement of man and beast, so there's no doubt He knows the day Tildy's payment is due." She looked at me sternly. "You'd better read some extra verses in the Bible, Carley Bimberg. I've taught you better than that."

I looked down at the table, feeling ashamed of my doubt. When it came to the Lord, Ma had no doubt, and if there was any chance of a miracle, she made the Lord responsible.

Pa smiled easily. He knew better than to enter the conversation when it came to Ma's beliefs. "Well, it's a miracle all right. If it wasn't for the money showing up the day before the payment is due that poor old widow would be thrown off her property and then I don't know what would happen to her."

"Yes, that's true," Ma said, her voice softening.

I nodded my head and ran my hand over Shiner's head. His fur was as smooth as buttermilk. It felt good in my hand.

Pa scooted his chair back and stretched. "Well, I've got some bookwork to do before I turn on the radio. The sooner I get at it the sooner I'll be through."

Ma got up. "You go ahead." Looking up at the pendulum clock on the wall, she shook her head. "I can't believe it's practically seven o'clock and I haven't even got the dishes washed and put away. That's the latest I've been in years." She turned to me "Carley, you put Shiner down and help me with the dishes. I'm behind and I want to make a few more pies before bedtime, too."

I started to put up a fuss. I wanted to go to my room and work on my B-29 model plane, but one glance at her warning eyes, and I knew there was no use. "All right, Ma," I said. "Let's hurry and get them done so the night isn't all gone."

Pa mussed my hair playfully. "You do what your Ma says. You've got plenty of time for other things."

"Your Pa's right," Ma said. "And after the dishes are done, you and I are going to sit down and read the Bible together. I don't want any boy of mine to be a doubter."

There goes my model building time, I thought to myself. When would I ever learn to keep my mouth shut? I stood up and started to collect the dishes, knowing there was no use arguing the point.

My rock made five skips. I smiled proudly. "I finally beat you!" I said to Troop, who was an expert at skipping rocks.

"That was a good rock you found, Carley. It was as flat as I've ever seen," Troop said.

One thing about Troop, he never got jealous. If you bettered him at something, he was the first one to give you the credit. That was just one of the things I liked about him. I suppose it was because he usually got the best of me. Like I said before, Troop could climb trees, run, swim, track, and everything better than any kid in town. I suppose if you're that good at everything important, you could afford to be generous once in awhile when someone bettered you. You'd know you were still good at all of those other things. He was sure lucky. He was born to be good at all of the important things in life.

My stomach ached a little as the heat slid through the willow leaves overhead. Troop, Shiner and I had just finished off six sandwiches, a half watermelon, a couple of slices of raisin cake, and a jug of fresh milk. We bulged at the seams.

I started getting real lazy. The cool shady spot beneath the old elm to my right seemed to be just begging me to crumple up there. I bounced one more rock across the creek, then plopped Shiner on my shoulder and went over to the tree. I laid myself on the ground, letting the cool breeze off the water wave over me. Shiner scampered around on my chest. He'd stand up, sniffing the catfishy smell, and then run up and down me, from the top of my head to my toes. It tickled but felt good at the same time. I sure was getting to love that little rascal.

Troop came over and laid down beside me. He stuck a blade of grass between his teeth and put his arms beneath his head, looking up to the sky.

"You believe in miracles, Troop?" I asked, lazily fondling Shiner's ear.

"I believe in the gods if that's what you mean," he said. "I believe in Manito."

"Gods?" I asked. "You mean God, don't you?"

"I mean gods. All of them. I believe in the sun god, rain god, and moon god. They all make miracles. After all, they make our crops grow and heal us when we're sick."

I looked over at him. I knew he was totally serious.

"We really believe in the same thing, though, don't we? I mean, no matter if you believe there's one or ten gods we still believe that they or He can do real powerful things."

Troop's eyes swung toward me. "Why are you talking about all of this, Carley? We never talked about this before. Why now?"

"Because some miracles have been happening right here in Belford," I answered thoughtfully.

Troop propped his head up with his hand. "What are you talking about? I haven't heard of any miracles here in Belford."

"Well, there's been some. My Pa told me about some going on right here." I hunched my shoulders. "Well, maybe not right here but close by; only four or five miles east of here."

Troop stared at me, saying nothing.

"You probably don't know her. Her name's 'Tildy Jorgenson and she lives on some dirt back roads four or five miles from Belford. She's as poor as a church mouse, as Pa says. In fact, Pa helps her out with a few free groceries now and then."

"Where do the miracles come in?" Troop asked impatiently.

"Well, it seems this poor old lady has a big debt on her farm. The bank is ready to make her move so they can take over. But lately, the past few months, right before her mortgage payment is due, she's been finding a sack full of money."

Troop's eyes got as big as saucers. "The gods are helping that old woman. It's sure as my father is Charlie Whitewater. You don't doubt it do you, Carley?" Troop's expression was dead serious. "Many Indians believe in Manito. The Kansa, Osage, Pottawatomie, Pawnee, and Wichita tribes that used to live in Kansas all believed in Manito."

I flopped Shiner up on my chest and petted him. He chattered like a squirrel. I didn't want to say anything to sound like a doubter. I do believe the Lord deals in miracles. Why, just us living is a miracle in itself. And every time I see a new born animal coming into the world, whether it's a newborn kitten or a kicking calf, I believe in the Lord's miracles. The green grass and the heaped up clouds and great sky are the miracles of the Lord. But, a sack of silver dollars— I just don't know. Somehow, I'm not sure the Lord deals in money like a banker or something. He'd more likely set a bushel of potatoes or turnips on her porch, I think.

I shook my head vigorously. "No. I don't doubt it. My Ma would skin me alive if I doubted it. I read through the whole chapter of Luke with her last night." I shook my head again. "No, sir, I'm not about to say I doubt it."

Troop looked at me close. I could tell by his squinty eyes he didn't believe me. He knew when I was fibbing.

"There's a way to prove it," Troop said quietly.

"You can't prove something like that."

"We could watch the miracle happen," he said, looking around as though he was worried someone would overhear.

"What are you talking about?"

Troop wiggled closer. "Well, you said the old lady always found the money the last day of the month because the payment was due on the first. Right?"

I nodded. "Right?"

"Well, all we have to do is wait until the last day of the month and go out there." His eyes sparkled. "We may see a real miracle out there at night."

"I raised my hand. "Hold on! You're not talking about me pulling that slat out from beneath my bed and putting it in the tree, are you?"

"Sure. Why not? It's worked so far, hasn't it?" Even the night of Darrell's initiation you got back up there without your Ma and Pa knowing anything about it, didn't you?"

"Yeah, that's true, but Ma is still wondering where that strange pair of overalls came from in the wash."

"But can you imagine," Troop said with a twinkle in his eye, "what Darrell's Ma is thinking, wondering where that strange apron came from?"

Troop and I looked at each other and folded up in a real gut-busting laugh. We hit each other's shoulders and bumped each other as tears ran down our cheeks, still seeing poor Darrell racing down that dirt road, wearing that lady's apron, his bare behind shining in the moonlight.

Shiner, wondering what all the whooping and hollering was about, stood up on his hind legs. He cocked his head toward Troop and then looked at me. He started running back and forth, not at all sure we weren't crazy.

Finally, we stopped laughing and, holding our aching ribs, gasped for breath.

"Boy, that was something. That sure was," I said.

Troop got all serious again. "Well, you didn't give me a straight answer. Are we going out there to see a miracle or not? This may be a once-in-a-lifetime chance."

I thought for a time. I knew he would talk me into it like he always did, and I thought I might as well save my energy. Slowly, I nodded my head. "All right, you win. I'll pull that old slat out once more." I shook my head. "Darnit, Troop, you can talk the bark off a tree."

Troop grinned. "Good. Now, you said the miracle always happens a day before the payment is due. "So Wednesday's the day. That's July 31st. That's the night of the miracle."

I looked into his eyes and shivers raced down my back. Something about an honest to goodness miracle made me all goose-pimply.

"It's spooky out here," I whispered, the sweat dripping off my nose. There wasn't a bit of breeze tonight.

"It's late. Must be close to two in the morning," Troop said.

I checked the pocketwatch Pa gave me. "Well, I ain't sitting up in this tree much longer. Every muscle in my body is squealing for mercy."

Troop nodded "I know. I feel the the same way. Let's give it another hour, and then if nothing happens, we'll climb down and go on home."

"We'll still have a long walk back. We'll be crawling in bed about the time the sun comes up. Then I'll have to crawl right back out again at six o'clock and start my chores. I'll be walking on my knees before the day is over."

"You can't hurry a miracle, Carley. The spirits have to be in the right mood. Manito can't be hurried." Troop looked around, his eyes wide. "Maybe just our being here has stopped the miracle from happening."

"That could be. All I know is, Shiner's getting real sleepy." I looked down at him nestled in the crook of my arm, his eyes shut and his nose tucked beneath my chin. It was cold and wet as usual. He was breathing deep and kind of purring like a cat.

I stretched, trying to get the kinks out of my legs. "I swear, I don't think I'll ever be able to stand straight and walk again."

Troop said nothing, staring right into the darkness. He never seemed to get tired. It was like the times Troop and I ran in a meadow for miles or climbed fifty trees straight up or swam across a big farm pond. He never panted and sputtered like I did. He always looked and acted as fresh as a daisy.

"Shhh!" Troop said, holding a finger to his lips. "I hear something."

I craned my neck one way and then the other. There was a pretty good moon, but still it looked pitch dark to me. I didn't see anything stirring at all. It was so hot it was hard to breathe. 'Tildy's house was pitch dark. I wondered how she slept so sound on the night when miracles happened. Gee, I'd be up all night peeking out the window. Of course, maybe she was so used to it by now, after all these months, that she didn't get all riled up. I mean, it might be like having a birthday every month or something. After a while, it wouldn't be special at all. It'd be just another day. Even cake and ice cream can become boring, I suppose.

Anyway, I trusted Troop. If he said he heard something then he heard something. He had ears like a wolf. He could hear a rabbit scamper across snow or grass blowing in the wind.

"I don't hear it," I whispered. "Where's it coming from?"

Troop nodded toward a wooded grove. I strained my eyes but could hear nothing.

"Something's there. I don't know what it is, but something's there," he said in a whisper.

Troop shook like a cold shiver was running up and down his spine. His eyes were as big as my fists beneath his straw hat. The way he acted made me feel all nervous. Shiner's head raised up and he cocked it from side to side. He got to his feet, staring in the exact direction Troop heard the sound. They both had ears and noses alike, that was sure. Troop was half animal and maybe Shiner had a little human in him, too.

Troop drew his breath in real quick. Like when you have your mouth too full and you start to choke. He drew back, pulling his hat way down over his eyes. "Manito, Manito, Manito," he said, looking away.

Shiner clucked, and scampered up my arm to my shoulder. There, he buried his head inside the collar of my shirt as though he didn't want to see anything.

There in the distance, looking like a huge black mountain, moved a figure or person...or something. The moon surrounded him in light, making it look even more spooky, kind of like a spirit. Then it started moving slowly toward 'Tildy's house.

"Manito, Manito, Manito," Troop repeated in a whisper as he peeked beneath the brim of his hat.

My adam's apple was up in the roof of my mouth. I couldn't say a word. I just sat there watching that huge, black figure come slowly forward one careful step at a time.

"It's a miracle, Carley," Troop gasped. "We are seeing a real miracle with our own eyes."

I stuck my head out through the thick leaves for a closer look.

"It is a god...maybe the god of wind, or rain, or the moon god or even Manito Himself..."

"Well, if it's a god," I said, "then he's riding the biggest buckskin you ever saw in your life."

"What?" Troop stuck his head out looking closer. "It's him!" Troop gasped. "

"It sure is. As sure as we're sitting up here all night. It sure is."

"But, what's he up to?"

"Troop, it doesn't take any real brainy person to guess that. Old Luke Webster is your miracle or god or whatever. That's all."

Both of us sat still as stones as he rode beneath the tree we were sitting in, proceeding to 'Tildy's front porch.

We watched him ride that buckskin right through the gate and right up to her front porch. There, he leaned over and dropped something. Troop and I swung around, looking at each other. By the sound of the jingling coins, it couldn't be anything else but a sack of silver dollars. Then he wheeled that big buckskin around and high-tailed it out of the yard and back down the road toward the grove of trees.

"But, why?" Troop asked, his mouth opened as wide as a cave. "Why would he do that? Luke Webster is supposed to be a bad man, a crazy man."

I didn't say anything. For once there was nothing to say. I looked at the cloud of dust settling back in the moonlit night. I thought of his old sister, Anna, who died a couple of months ago. Maybe Luke thought in some way he was doing something for her. Who knows? But one thing was for sure: Luke Webster made a strange god. But, when you think of it, you don't have to be a god to make miracles happen.

Chapter 10

The month of August was the craziest summer month I've ever seen. Usually, everything turns brown and crisp, and deep cracks pull the ground apart. Usually, all of Ma's zinnias wilt, and every blade of grass in our yard burns up. This August was real different. Every day, for the last two weeks, it had rained. And not just an inch or such, but real gully-washers. It'd stop and the sun would peek through. Then about time the sun starts to set, the clouds would all bunch up again, lightning would tear through the skies, thunder would shake the house, and the rain would fall again in torrents. Our garden was like a swamp. The beans and potatoes were drowned. People all over town had their sump pumps going to get rid of the water in their basements. Old farmers scratched their heads in wonder. This was the darndest month on record for August. Many farmers hadn't gotten into their fields for weeks. When some of them tried, they got bogged down with mud clear up to the hubs on their wheels. People ran with umbrellas over their heads and wore yellow slickers and galoshes. Kids in town had fun because the gutters were filled and it was great to romp around in the water. There was nothing but water, puddles, and mud everywhere.

All of that wasn't harmful. I mean, even though it got real boring, life could go on. Pa stayed open and even though business slowed down, he still turned a profit, he said. Ma did a whole lot of sewing. She mended every hole in Pa's and my socks and pants that we had. She even started doing some embroidering on some tea towels. I got real tired staying in and I know Shiner did. He'd prance around in the house, crawling up on the table when Ma wasn't looking, tasting the sugar in the sugar bowl and pinching off little hunks of fresh baked bread. It was a good thing she never caught him, because if she did, there might have been one skinned coon or at the very least one wet one, because out he would've gone back into the rabbit hutch. Whenever I caught him up on the table, I'd snatch him away from there fast, hurrying to see where Ma was. More than once, I took the blame for the overturned sugar bowl and hunks of bread missing from the crusts.

Shiner was pesky at times, I knew that. But he was sure good company on those long rainy days when I'd curl up on the couch, reading *Moby Dick* or the *Last of the Mohicans*. He was always laying in my lap, walking along my shoulders, or sleeping on my feet. I couldn't imagine how it would be without him. It seemed like Shiner had been with me forever. I knew I never wanted to be without him, that's for sure. He was better than any dog could ever be. He wasn't just a pet; he was my friend.

And then the news came that the Big Blue River was out of its banks and raging through corn and wheat fields, tearing away precious top soil, making gulleys and destroying crops. The business part of the town would be safe, people said, but the residential parts of town might be in for a real flood. If this rain didn't stop, we'd all be wading in some deep water.

All afternoon, Ma and I put up stuff on chairs and boxes. We carried things Ma thought were " precious" up the stairs. Things like pictures, her ma's china cabinet and the old rocker her grampa used years ago. I swear, we worked all afternoon. The house looked like we were moving or something.

Ma had a couple of guys come in and put her ice box up on blocks. If the flood waters did come into the house, it'd have to get real high to hurt any of our things. Pa came home that night with a worried look on his face. He said the Big Blue was expected to flood real bad because of the heavy rains upstream. It was supposed to crest around noon the next day. Ma shook her head and instructed the both of us to say some extra prayers to the Lord when we went to sleep that evening. He was the only one who could help us now, she said. Pa agreed but said he'd sit up in case it got real bad before morning. At least, he said, he was glad Belford was built on a hill, so the store would be safe. That was one thing to be thankful for.

That night, I laid in bed looking out at the jagged spears of light shooting through the sky. Heavy drops of rain pelted my window. Everything smelled musty and damp like mildew. Shiner cuddled next to me, his nose poked beneath the pillow. I'll bet he was glad he was here instead of outside in all of that mess, I thought. Glancing down, Shiner looked as content as a cat sleeping there beside me.

My room lit up as lightning charged through the sky. It looked as if the rain could go on forever. I sighed, closing my eyes. There wasn't anything I or anybody could do about it. Only God could stop it now. It was up to Him.

That morning at breakfast both Ma and Pa were quiet. I could tell by their worried looks that there was going to be trouble. Pa commented about joining up with some men to try to sand bag the banks of the Blue, but he doubted if it would do any good at this stage. He told Ma that there would probably be a bunch of men along later to lift whatever we hadn't got up off the floor to higher ground.

After breakfast he pulled on his galoshes, slicker, and hat, turned his head away from the wind, and went through the door out into the downpour. Ma shook her head weakly and started picking up the dishes.

I was on the eleventh chapter of *Moby Dick* when someone pounded on the front door. Shiner's ears perked up. He rushed to the door and stood on his hind legs, pawing it. I thought it was the men to move our belongings. Ma rushed in, drying her hands on a dish towel, opened the door, and practically pulled the party standing on the porch inside. A gust of wind and rain tore through the door, coating me way over on the opposite side of the room wih a wet film.

Troop stood there dripping like a drowned rat. His long hair lay pasted to his head. I don't think he owned a raincoat. All he had on was a jacket, overalls and oversized hip boots. He shook his straw hat.

"My goodness, Brian, what on earth are you doing out on a day like this? Don't you know we could be in for a bad flood any minute?"

I wrinkled my nose when Ma called Troop Brian. She always called him that.

"I'm sorry for getting your floor wet, Mrs. Bimberg," Troop said. He was always polite to adults. In fact, when I think about it, Troop was always polite to everybody.

Shiner stood on his hind legs, begging Troop to pick him up. He chattered for attention, and at last Troop looked down and picked him up. That little critter was pleased as punch when Troop nuzzled his fur lovingly. That coon sure did like attention.

"Never you mind, Brian. You get out of that coat and pants and pull those boots off. I want you dry before you catch your death."

Troop looked over at me for help. I knew he wasn't about to take his clothes off in front of my Ma. He'd rather die of pneumonia first.

"Maybe Troop...er, Brian is going right back out, Ma." I looked over at Troop, winking.

Troop nodded vigorously. "Yes, ma'am that's what I'm going to do. My mother sent me up town to get information about the flood. You see, our house is in a very low section of town and we're almost certain to be flooded. My Pa's at work. A lot of the track needs repairing. He's been working all night."

"And your mother is home alone." Ma shook her head. "Why, that's not right. I'll go right over there and bring her here. I imagine she's just scared to death and I don't blame her. She's never been in a flood in Belford before. It's really scary if you don't know what to expect."

Before Troop answered, Ma had her scarf tied around her head, her raincoat on, and was reaching for the door knob. She turned. "Now, Carley, you be sure that Brian is dried out. You can make him some cocoa, too. That'll warm him up. I'll be right back after I fetch Mrs. Whitewater. I'll not have that poor woman there all by herself. I'll just not have it."

I nodded. One thing about Ma: when she decided something you might as well give her her head. I had to admit that I was proud of her, as I often was, because she was always ready to help someone who needed it. She was some Ma and I was one lucky kid for having her. Before another word was said, she pushed herself out the door into the wind and driving rain.

"Your Ma is real kind, Carley. I thank her for that. Especially, when my Ma is shy and doesn't understand English and all."

"I'm sure Ma is glad to do it." I motioned for Troop to sit down beside the wood stove glowing red with heat. "If you want to get out of your clothes I can go get you a blanket." I started getting up, but Troop stopped me with his hand.

"No. I'm all right. I have to leave anyway."

"What're you talking about? You just got here out of the rain."

"I told Ma I'd find out about the chances of flooding and that's what I'm going to do. I'm on my way out to the river. I also thought I could help with the sand bags."

I felt like a lazy hound. Here I was snug as a bug reading *Moby Dick* and there was all the men in town and probably a lot of the boys helping to hold back the Big Blue. Why hadn't I thought of it before?

"You're right, Troop. That's where we both should be. My Pa's been out all day helping people sandbagging the banks. I'm old enough. It's crazy for me to be staying in here like a baby." Jumping off the couch, I went to the rack to get my raincoat. "If you don't mind, I'll go along with you."

"What will your Ma say, Carley? Are you going to wait and ask her?"

I poked my arms in my slicker. "Criminy, no. She wouldn't let me go if I did. Besides, Pa will probably be around there and I can ask him. I'm not about to stay in here like this."

Troop looked doubtful. "I don't know. Maybe you'd better wait and ask. Your Ma will be mighty worried."

I hurried to Pa's desk. "I tell you what. To ease your worry and everything, I'll write her a note telling her where I went." I tore a piece of paper off of Pa's note pad and scratched out a hurried note. "There! Does that make you feel better?"

Troop nodded. "Yes, I guess so. But, I still don't think she's going to like it. It could be dangerous out there by the river."

"Your Ma is letting you go, isn't she? Besides, both Mas can comfort each other." I stuck out my chest. "We're both almost men now, Troop. It's our duty to help the town when it needs it."

I pulled on my overshoes and started to the door. Troop put Shiner down, but Shiner scrambled up my arm and perched on my shoulder. We both laughed. "At least leave Shiner here, Carley. He'll get soaked out there."

I thought about him getting into things while I was gone. I knew he'd head for the sugar bowl and Ma's fresh baked bread. Or he might scramble up her curtains and snag them real bad. Or he might get into the cupboards and break a bunch of dishes or get in the closets and cause damage. If I wasn't here there's no telling what he'd get into. I shook my head and petted Shiner on my shoulder. "No," I said, "Shiner's going with me. He'll be safe. I'll watch him real close."

"I guess you know what you're doing," Troop said, pulling the door open against the wet wind.

The rain came down in grey sheets. Every three steps we took, the wind blew us back two. I never saw wind and rain this bad. Shiner was tucked warmly away in my raincoat pocket. I felt the weight of him on the right side of my coat. Every once in a while his nose and black eyes poked out and he'd sniff the wind and then pull back, glad to be where it was dry and warm.

It took over an hour to get out to the river bridge. I couldn't believe what I saw. The water was higher than I ever saw it. When you threw rocks from the bridge it took a while before they hit water. Now the water was so high, you could reach down and touch it. That is, if you dared to. It was rushing madly downstream. Treacherous whirlpools churned and swirled. Large branches and timbers rushed beneath us. The water was muddy and foam coated. The gypsy encampment was underwater some four or five feet. Men rushed here and there filling sand bags. Trucks and cars set stuck in mud up to their bumpers. Everybody looked alike with their yellow hoods and slickers. I couldn't see Pa in all the crowd.

Troop and I went to work lifting sand bags in a chain of men. Before an hour was over, my back ached like all get out, but I wasn't about to complain. Some of them had been here all night working. Troop stood beside me, lifting away, not saying one word or complaining. I knew he wouldn't. He never did. He just went about his business. I guess he felt a lot better knowing his Ma was safe with my Ma.

I took Shiner out of my coat pocket and allowed him to run about. He was more curious than ever with all of the goings on.

After the second hour, Mr. Mercer tapped Troop and me on the shoulders, telling us to take a break. We didn't argue, just stepped out of line, and two others took our places. From where we stood, we heard the roar of the rushing water. One guy handed us tin cups of scalding hot coffee. It made both of us feel real grown up.

"You two drowned rats doing your good deed for the day?"

Troop and I turned, seeing a wet freckled face looking out from under a grey raincoat hood.

"Don't see you giving anybody a hand, Mick," I said, trying to ignore him.

"That's for chumps, Bimberg. They don't give you no pay. Mick Fuller don't work if there's no pay."

"It's up to you what you do, Mick. Just stay out of the way, then," I said coldly.

Mick shook his staff at me. "You'd better watch yourself, Bimberg, or you'll find your teeth at the bottom of the river. I can hang around here if I want to. And if I don't want to work, that's all right, too. It's a free country."

"Yeah, that's right." I turned my back to him.

I knew that would really get to him. One thing Mick Fuller didn't stand for was someone to turn his back to him. I knew that would make him good and mad.

He rushed around to the other side. "Where's that stupid coon of yours?" He looked down, nudging Devil. "Probably too chicken to get out in the rain. Is that it?"

"He's here, Mick. He's mixing in with the men." I looked around for him.

"Sure he is. Sure he is. I don't see no sign of that mangy critter. I know if he was around here my dog would tear him apart, after what that critter did to him."

Just then, Shiner came up to us, chattering as he approached. Devil started to whine and backed away. Mick's eyes squinted with hate.

"Well, look who's here, Mick," I said, grinning? Old Shiner wouldn't miss helping for the world."

118

"Helping? Sure, helping. He's doing nothing but getting a free ride."

Troop and I decided to ignore Mick. There wasn't any use trying to talk to him. No matter what we said he always said the opposite. That was Mick Fuller for you.

We handed our coffee cups back to a lady beneath a tarpaulin tent and went back in line to lift sandbags. Both Troop and I felt older and taller, drinking coffee like men and doing a man's job. It was a good feeling.

Mick, Frank, and Lowell were throwing rocks into the charging current. I think the three of them would stand there and let the whole town go under before they'd lift one finger. There's no explaining some people. Even though my back and arms were tired, it was a good tired. I hope Ma understood. I hope Pa would help explain it to her. It was something Troop and I had to do. Gunny sacks were filled and the tops tied. They were handed down a long line of men from one to another and then stacked to ward off the raging waters of the Big Blue.

It was just getting dark when it happened. My blood still turns to ice when I think about it. The scream put the hair on the back of my neck straight on end. Everyone on line dropped the sandbags and rushed to the bridge. Troop and I ran with them. I couldn't believe what I saw. There was Mick all red-faced, snot streaming out of his nose, crying his eyes out, and pointing down at the waters below.

"What's the trouble, young man?" Mr. Mercer asked. He was the head of the crew of men stacking sand bags.

Mick's face was so red, it looked like it was ready to explode. "Down there! Down in the water. My dog...he slipped and fell off the bridge. He fell into the river!"

Every eye turned toward the swirling, bucking water. Some men leaned way over the railing trying to get a good look.

"I don't see him, young fella!" Mr. Mercer screamed. The roar of the water was so deafening we could hardly hear him.

"Down there!" Mick shouted. "He fell down there! He was running along the bridge and skidded on some rock and mud and fell right in. I went to grab him but he fell."

The men who were stretched over the railing looked up and shook their heads. Mr. Mercer put his arm around Mick's shoulders. I could tell by the look on his wet face that the news wasn't good. "Now, young fella, don't get your hopes up. That water is twenty-five to thirty feet deep and running faster than I've seen it in forty years. I don't want to give you bad news, but if your dog fell in there he doesn't have much of a chance."

Roughly, Mick pulled away from Mr. Mercer. "You don't know what you're talking about. My dog's a good swimmer. He'll get himself out of there."

"It takes more than a good swimmer to get out of water like that. Nothing could survive that kind of water. Best you go over to the tent and get yourself a cup of hot coffee and one of the men will take you home. I'm afraid there's no hope for your dog. He's a goner in that water."

Troop and I looked sadly from one to the other. As much as we disliked Mick and Devil, we didn't want anything like this to happen. No matter what a rotten kid Mick was, the one thing in this world he cared for was Devil. That accounted for something, we decided. We also knew there wasn't anything anyone could do. Like Mr. Mercer said, anyone or anything that fell in that water was a goner for sure.

Mick sobbed, wiping at his eyes and nose with the sleeve of his raincoat. He walked, shoulders slumped, toward the tent, Frank and Lowell following. I looked after them through the rain. It was strange not seeing Devil tagging right along beside Mick as usual. Troop and I stayed on the bridge feeling pretty sad. Leaning down, I petted Shiner on the head. It was a good feeling to see him safe.

"I guess that's it for Devil, huh, Troop?" I asked.

He nodded. "He won't be hurting any more cats and dogs and growling at people, that's for sure."

"I never liked that dog, but I wish this hadn't happened."

"I know what you mean. No dog deserves that. Not even Devil," Troop said.

I sighed. "Well, I guess we'd better get back in line. There's nothing anybody can do."

"Yeah, I suppose so." Troop leaned over the railing peering downstream into the water. He stayed there for a time, staring at the same spot. "Carley!" he cried. "I think I see him!"

"What?" I ran over and leaned over the railing. I couldn't see a thing through the dark and rain.

"Over there, about two hundred yards downstream. I think I see him. He's trapped between two logs. I barely see his head. That mane is what shows him up."

"You really see him? Is there any way to get him out?"

"I don't know. We've got to get closer. I know one thing: once that log lets loose there'd be no chance for him. He'd be in open waters and he'd drown for sure."

"Let's get down there and have a look," I said. I propped Shiner on my shoulder and started running to where Troop was pointing.

"Wait! Shouldn't we tell Mick? Shouldn't we tell him that Devil's down there?" yelled Troop.

I called back over my shoulder. "No. In case those logs get caught in the stream, there's no use giving him hope. We probably will get there too late anyway."

Troop nodded. "I see what you mean. Let's give it a try!" He ran up alongside me.

Troop and I sank in mud up to our ankles. It made sucking sounds when we pulled our feet out. The going was real slow. In the distance, beneath the roar of the river, I heard Devil whine fearfully. For once, he wasn't lording himself over a helpless smaller victim. He was in a bad position and he knew it. Luckily for him, he was entangled in some branches lodged in brush that kept them from being swept downstream.

Troop breathed hard beside me. It was the first time I ever heard him out of breath. "I don't know, Carley. That's taking a real chance trying to get to him. One slip and we'd be goners for sure. Maybe we'd better run back up there and get some help."

I pointed to the pile of brush bobbing up and down in the swift current. "There isn't time, Troop," I yelled. "By the time we get up there and they get back, that whole pile is gonna be pushed on downstream and Devil'll be swept under the current and whirlpools. His only chance is for us to try and get him now." I nodded. "I know that Mick is sometimes the lowest thing on earth, but Devil is still an animal, a living being. We can't stand here and let him drown." The rain stung my face. I looked close at Troop. He had no expression on his face, as usual. Finally, he nodded.

"Let's go," I said. " There's not much of a chance, but if there's any at all, we'd better take it now before it's too late." I lowered Shiner to the muddy bank. "Stay here, Shiner, by this tree. It's good, solid ground. Just wait for me, buddy, okay?" Shiner cocked his head at me, chattered a bit, but stayed put. "Good, Shiner. Take it easy. I'll be right back."

Slapping Troop on the back, we started toward Devil. We didn't take more than ten steps when we fell into water over our chests. I grabbed some branches, pulling myself forward. Troop was beside me spitting water. Another three steps and we couldn't touch bottom. The current swept past me, pulling me from the branches. I looked into Troop's glassy eyes. It could have been fear I saw there. I don't know. But I knew I was just about as scared as I've ever been in my life.

My heart leaped into my throat. "Watch out!" I cried. "There's a big log floating right toward us!"

We both let loose of the branches at the same time, diving beneath the water. I was pulled into a whirlpool, a huge suction machine, pulling me down and down into a watery grave. Fear knifed through me. I held my breath as long as I could, until I swallowed a gulp of cold river water. My thoughts were with Troop; had he been caught in the same whirlpool? I thought of Ma and Pa and how sad they'd be if I didn't make it. My hood was snatched off my head and I caught a glimpse of it being swept under. I coughed and choked, but I wasn't about to give up. We Bimbergs never give up until the end. I started repeating a few prayers Ma taught me, saying them real fast-like. It was as dark as a cave under water. But, miracles do happen, as Ma says. I bobbed out of the whirlpool and found myself right in the middle of the river, being tossed around like a feather. The weight of the raincoat pulled me down. Quickly, while the water sent me racing downstream, I stripped out of the coat and, let it float away. My head hit against branches and logs. It stung and throbbed. I knew the end had come until a hand reached out as I was speeding by and pulled me to a log. It was Troop holding on to the log right next to Devil. For a minute, I draped myself over the log, vomiting river water. I was as weak as a newborn kitten.

"Hold on, Carley. Hold on! We're going to make it. Just hold on!" Troop screamed.

I smiled my gratitude to Troop. I was too weak to say anything. Slowly, I pulled myself up on the log to a sitting position.

"We...we made it, Troop," I gasped, water seeping out of the corners of my mouth. "Now, all we have to do is get hold of Devil and pull him to the bank before this bunch of brush lets loose and goes sweeping downstream."

We reached down, pulling with all our strengths, finally managing to get Devil up on the log. He stood there soaked and shaking, whimpering with fear. The logs lurched beneath us and we knew they were ready to be torn loose by the current.

"We've got to get back right now, Carley," Troop yelled. "It's ready to give way. If it does, we're all goners." The pile of brush shook beneath us.

"You're right. We've got to go right now."

The brush pile lurched again and Devil whined fearfully. I grabbed a hunk of Devil's mane. Troop grabbed another hunk and we started pulling him toward the bank. Devil whined all the way, but he didn't struggle. He must have known that if we let go there was no way he was going to come through this alive.

Just as we cleared the brush pile, it pulled away and was swept downstream in the violent current. We made it by seconds. Troop and I moaned with weariness, pulling that heavy dog to shore.

We stumbled onto the bank, falling face down in the mud. We laid there for two or three minutes, too tired to move. The rain continued to coat us, but we were alive. The three of us struggled back toward the bridge through the knee deep mud.

Chapter 11

As we trudged up to the bridge, the men and boys came running and screaming in disbelief. There we were muddy and drenched, but very much alive. Mick stood there for a few moments, the rain pelting his face, looking as though he didn't believe his eyes. He thought that Devil was a sure goner. Finally, he threw down his staff and ran toward us. He fell to his knees and placed his arms about Devil's neck. He didn't say anything for a long time. Finally, he looked up and tears of gratitude were streaming down his face.

The men were pounding us on the back with congratulations. Everybody was celebrating. Troop and I felt at least nine feet tall.

Pa, however, had a scowl on his face. I knew I'd get it when I got home. He was not happy at the chance Troop and I took getting Devil out of the river. I swallowed hard when I saw that warning frown on his face. But, at least Pa was going to wait until we got home. He wasn't about to take anything away from our proud feeling right now and embarrass us. Pa was always fair, I've got to admit that.

Finally, Mick got to his feet. He looked me straight in the eyes and tried to clear his throat. "Carley, I'm much obliged to you and Troop for saving Devil. I didn't think I would ever see him again. I still can't believe that he's okay." He stuck out his hand to shake.

I couldn't believe it. I was actually shaking Mick Fuller's hand. It was one of the strangest days of my life. He then turned to Troop and shook his hand.

"Well, Mick," I said, "he's soaked to the skin and shaking like a leaf in a strong wind, but I think he'll be fine."

Everyone around who heard it over the roar of the water laughed loud and beat us on the backs once again.

Then they all returned to their jobs of stacking sand bags, leaving Troop, Mick, Devil and me on the bridge.

It just occurred to me in all of the excitement that I hadn't seen Shiner for an hour or so. My stomach got all fluttery with panic. I looked down at the wild, churning water and felt a little sick.

"Oh, Troop, I forgot about Shiner! We've got to go back down to the bank. He's still down there. I only pray he didn't get into the water and was swept downstream."

"He's too smart to do that, Carley," Troop assured me. Troop and I started to leave the bridge.

"Wait!" Mick called. "Devil and I want to go with you to hunt for Shiner. That's the least we can do."

I nodded gratefully. We could use all the help we could get.

The four of us started trudging through the mud once again. We were ignored by the men on the bridge. They still had to think about preventing the flood waters from coming out of the banks. I looked around and called Shiner's name. Troop and Mick did the same thing. There was no sign of him.

We walked for over ten minutes, looking out toward the water and searching the banks. I could feel myself getting real shaky. I couldn't believe that Shiner would just run away like that. The worst thing would be that he got caught in the river water. I knew he was a good swimmer, but no one could swim in that water. Not even Shiner.

"I'll say a prayer to Manito, Carley," Troop told me under his breath. "He is always there to protect humans and animals."

I nodded, but I couldn't say anything.

Troop, Mick, and I continued to trudge through miles of knee deep mud. Everything along the banks was laying flat from the tremendous force of the rain. A few times, we slipped and fell face first into the muck, coming up covered from head to toe. Big chunks of the bank were being washed away, and the river had new twists and bends now.

It wouldn't be as familiar as it used to be to us. Troop and I knew every inch of these banks from summers of cat-fishing.

I knew if I pulled my feet out of one more mud hole I'd collapse. I crumpled to the mud, unable to go one more step until I rested.

Troop placed his mud-coated hands on his hips. His eyes showed like two peep holes through his muddy face. "Carley, let's keep going. We've only been searching for a couple of hours."

I pushed myself up, draping my arm around his shoulders, and looked into the distance. Mick and Devil had gone on ahead.

"Hey! Hey, Bimberg! Hey!" Mick shouted in the distance.

Troop and I swung our attention to Mick who was hunting around a bend in the river. We saw him wave his hat in the air.

"Mick's found something," Troop said.

I started running, not waiting to hear Troop finish his sentence.

Mick waved his hat in the air again. I knew he was excited. My heart was pumping like crazy.

Devil was at the foot of a little sick-looking tree all bent over from the terrible storm. Most of its leaves were torn off or in shreds from the force.

Troop ran up beside me and pointed. "There's something up in that sorry tree over there or Devil wouldn't be barking." He squinted his eyes. "In fact, I see something, or two somethings."

"What is it?" I gasped.

"I don't know. It's too far away. But whatever it is, it's driving Devil crazy." He really wants to get to them."

My heart started pounding. What would be the thing Devil wanted to get to most of all in the world? I asked myself. A coon, naturally! A coon nearly drowned him a few weeks ago. A coon made a royal monkey out of him. That dog wanted to get hold of that coon in the worst way. That's for sure.

I ran toward Devil as fast as those heavy boots would take me. I slipped and slid all over the place. More than once I got up with a mouthful of mud. For once, I beat Troop to the tree. My breath spurted out in loud gusts. Devil was going crazy, barking his head off at the base of the tree.

I put my hand up to visor my eyes and looked clear up to the top of the tree. The rain blurred my vision, but I saw something. There it was. A rag-tag face with two pitch black eyes looking fearfully through some leaves at me. It was a raccoon all right, but was it Shiner?

My eyes swung to another branch, sighting another one. Sure as the world, there were two coons in that tree. Both were shaking with fright, looking fearfully down at that red maned dog snarling at them from below.

Troop saw what I saw. "Is it? Is one of them Shiner? Can you tell?"

I shook my head. "I can't tell a thing from down here. I'm going up there to see for sure."

Mick and Troop gave me a boost and I hoisted myself up to a limb. Once on that limb, I looked up through the branches. I still couldn't tell a thing. Looking down, I shook my head. My boots made me slip all over the place, so I pulled them off and let them drop to the mud below. Mick got Devil quieted down, his hand buried deep in that red mane.

One limb and then another. Up and up I went. The branches swayed. One of them creaked beneath my feet. Peering up through the foliage, I saw one coon scampering along a limb trying to escape me. My heart sank to my feet. It wasn't Shiner. There was no scar from the trap on its hind leg. My eyes scanned the branches for the other coon. I saw the black eyes peering through the branches, looking terrified. The flood waters had made both animals terribly afraid and I knew I could be bitten badly. Holding my breath, I pulled myself to another branch, just under the poor creature. It yipped fearfully and its hind feet slipped off the branch and dangled above me, as it clung to the tree

with its front paws. There were the scars of the trap on its hind leg. Shiner! Before I yelled, I gave a quick thank you to God or Manito, whoever had watched over Shiner.

"It's him!" I yelled. "I've found him. He's up here in the top branch of this old tree."

Troop and Mick yelled their heads off and Devil started barking again. Their screams and whoops echoed across the river.

"Shiner, it's me," I said softly. "Come on, boy." I whistled. "Come on down. It's me. I've come to take you home." Those two black eyes and pointed wet nose stuck through the leaves looking right at me. I knew right away that he recognized me. He chattered joyfully.

"Come on, boy. Come on, Shiner," I said. "Just crawl down here and I'll take you the rest of the way. Don't worry about Devil. He's not going to bother you."

I didn't think about it until later, but if it hadn't been for Devil, I wouldn't have found him. It was Devil who led me to Shiner, as sure as the world turns.

I reached up as far as I could, my arm stretching clear out of my sleeve. My fingertips touched his nose. He was smelling me to be sure. He chattered softly. Slowly, carefully, he came down into my arms. I felt every bone in his body through his matted wet hair. I nuzzled that little fella and he whimpered and put his nose in my ear as he always did when he showed me affection.

"Shiner, you little rascal. Why did you run away? You knew I'd be back to get you."

"Did you get him, Carley?" Troop called.

"Yeah, I got him and I'm coming down. Be sure to hold on to Devil real tight. I don't want to scare him any more than he's scared right now. Okay?"

"I'm holding Devil, Bimberg. Just bring him down," Mick said.

As we petted and fawned over Shiner, I saw him look back to the top of the tree to that other coon staring back at him.

Chapter 12

The sun had broken through the heavy clouds the next day, and the water started to go down. Belford had been saved. Everything settled down into a routine summer once again. I tried stretching each day out just as far as it'd go because I knew that old school bell would be clanging one of these days real soon.

Troop and I hurried our morning chores so we could get to the fish bank early. Those bullheads were so fat and sassy, they'd just about jump right out of the creek into our laps. Many times, we'd bring strings of them home, numbering fifteen to twenty, and Ma would cook them up for us. Catfish, fried potatoes, cream peas, homemade bread with churned butter, and piping-hot apple pie. Mmm-mmm, nothing was as good as that. My mouth waters just thinking about it. Ma always cooked that combination, just like when she had fried chicken, mashed potatoes, corn, homemade bread, and cherry cobbler. It always went together. She was the best cook in all of Riley County. Heck, probably the whole state for that matter. Nobody could outdo her in baking. Nobody at all.

Mick and his gang weren't after us like they once were. He wasn't my closest friend or anything, but at least he didn't look at me nose to nose with those grey, beady eyes of his, asking for a fight every time we met. Devil was still beating up cats and dogs, but Mick pulled him away from people when he started showing those sharp teeth. That was a change. If a person changed too much, too fast, it'd be a shock to his system, I suppose. Mick sure didn't want that.

Not much happens around small towns in the summer. Just the free picture shows on Saturday nights, flying chicken contests during the Fourth of July, church picnics, and ice cream socials. But nothing spectacular; nothing at all. A guy kind of "lazed" his way through this part of the summer. That was all right with me. It seemed that the older I got, the downright lazier I felt. Pa said it was because of my bones stretching every which way, growing too fast or something. Sometimes, I'd get up in the morning and pull on my pants and I swear I must've stretched another two or three inches during the night. Those cuffs kept climbing up my shinbones every day. Pretty soon they'd be clear to my knees. Ma always shook her head in wonder. She couldn't believe how I was climbing right out of my clothes.

Luke was still pulling miracles on old Tildy Jorgenson. Only Troop and I knew that he and not the Lord was responsible. We felt real important knowing that secret. We weren't about to tell a solitary soul what we saw that night. We knew Luke wanted it that way. When you think about it, maybe the Lord did have His hand in it. I mean, after all, He was the one who made Luke think about it, so maybe He was responsible, after all... It was too much for a kid's mind. Sometimes, I'd lay in bed with Shiner across my chest and ponder deep things like that. Before I'd go to sleep, I'd get all dizzy just thinking about it. It was way too much for me, way too much.

Speaking of Shiner and all: He changed after I brought him back from the river that day. I can't explain it, but he just wasn't himself. I noticed it right off. He'd either be real ornery or he'd be as droopy as the last rose of summer. Sometimes, I'd go out to his cage and he'd have left fish heads. They used to be his favorite. When we went out fishing, he used to jump around after butterflies and grasshoppers, but now he'd lay under a tree in the shade all curled up in a ball. And then sometimes he'd be just the opposite and be as ornery as they came. He'd chase the hens around the pen so much they wouldn't lay for

132

days. A few times I found him hanging from Ma's wash on the line. Or he'd get on the table and take big hunks out of the homemade bread. You just didn't know what to expect. He was always mischievous, but this was way beyond that.

Once, when Pa was out in the "little house" as Ma politely called our outdoor toilet, Shiner got on top of the roof, running back and forth. Pa didn't know what the sound was. He got so worried and upset he raised right up before finishing his business. He came out of there hollering and shaking his fist at Shiner up there on the roof. I thought for sure he was going to tell me to get rid of him. I'd just about die if that would happen.

I spent a whole lot of my time watching Shiner and keeping him out of trouble. One morning I woke up and looked down, expecting to see him curled close to me like he always was. He was nowhere around. I got worried right away. I hitched up my pants, not bothering with shirt and shoes, and tiptoed down the steps as quiet as I could. I breathed easier when I realized that Ma and Pa weren't up yet. It was just the crack of dawn. Everything was quiet except for Pa snoring in the bedroom. Shiner wasn't in the living room and he wasn't in the parlor. Where could that scamp be? I asked myself worriedly.

I crept into the kitchen and looked around from the doorway. My heart fell to my feet. There he was in Ma's flour bin, coated from head to toe in dusty white film. As if that wasn't bad enough, he ran and rolled over the floor and table, climbing the curtains leaving flour everywhere.

When I stepped through the doorway, he looked up with those shiny black eyes. He knew right off he was caught. I placed my hands on my hips and bit into my lip, afraid I'd holler a cuss word right then and there. Jumping out of the bin, he ran over to me and raised up on his hind legs, trying to apologize. I leaned over, grabbed him by the scruff of the neck, marched him out to the rabbit hutch, closed the door and hooked it. Shiner ran back and forth, chattering woefully, but I was determined to show him once and for all who was the boss. I turned once before I got to the screen door to see his flour coated face plead for me to take him out. Even though I felt sorry for him, I knew it was for his own good.

I was only half done cleaning when Ma got up. She shook her head right away knowing what had happened. She pitched right in helping me clean up before Pa finished shaving so the place would be presentable. She knew he'd ban him from the house forever after this. I've got a pretty good Ma, if I do say so myself.

Ma and I canned summer pickles until they came out of our ears- one hundred and ten quarts. I saved the biggest cucumber, a four-pounder, to enter in the produce section of the fair. Ma's pickles always got ribbons at the Riley County Fair and that big cucumber had a chance too. Two days before the fair, she baked bread, cinnamon rolls, apple and cherry pies, and chocolate cakes like crazy. You could smell the baking clear out to the garden. It smelled great and made my mouth water from morning until night. Everything was proudly lined up on the kitchen table. The smell of baking was everywhere, even in our clothes.

I stood guard over that table like a soldier guarding a secret weapon. No way was I going to let Shiner near that table. Ma worked too hard and too long to have anything happen. But strangely enough, he didn't even come close to the table. He was calmer now. He was even sort of melancholy. He'd go to the screen door at night and stand on his hind legs peering into the darkness. I don't know what was wrong with him. His eyes always seemed to be searching.

The day of the County Fair was exciting. This was always my favorite day of the whole summer. The Rydell Amusement Troupe always came to town, erecting dangerous, dizzying rides of all sorts: ferris wheels, swings, merry-go-rounds, and the Octopus, to name a few. I could ride on them forever. And then there were games of chance where you'd throw rings over bottles, knock down cans, scoop up wonderful prizes with toy cranes. You'd win a kewpie doll with sequins and bright feathers, or great plaster- of- Paris statues of snarling dogs and rearing horses. And there was always an artist who could paint a whole outdoor scene with beautiful colors in less than five minutes. I never did figure how he could do such a thing. That took great talent.

Shiner perched on my shoulder while I stood with Troop, watching guys a few years older than us trying to ring the bell by hitting this machine with a heavy wooden mallet. They'd rub dirt on their hands, flex their muscles, and grunt like crazy. Sometimes the gauge would only go up a little and they'd get real red-faced. You could tell they were trying to show off for their girl-friends. "How stupid," I whispered to Troop. "Who'd want to show off just for some dumb girls?" (Little did I know I'd be doing the same thing myself next summer.) A stout man wearing an undershirt and jeans stepped up to ring the bell. He had a fat cigar clamped between his puffy lips. The muscles in his arms and shoulders bulged and glistened with sweat. Picking up the mallet with one hand, he whammed it down, nearly pushing that bell clear off the stand. Proud as a peacock, he strutted his stuff to the cheering crowd, then turned and blew cigar smoke right in my face. He grinned down at me, showing snaggly, stained teeth.

"Hey, boy, where'd you get that coon there on your shoulder?" He reached out. "Let me see him," he said.

Before I could step aside, he pulled Shiner from my shoulder, plopping him on his own shoulder. He grinned, parading up and down with Shiner, while the crowd laughed and clapped. My face was beet-red, I was so mad.

135

For one thing, he had no right pulling Shiner away from me like that and for another thing I didn't like him at all. I tapped his arm.

"Hey, mister, can you give Shiner back to me now?" I asked politely.

He grinned. "Shiner?" he said. "Is that this little guy's name? Can he do any tricks?" He looked at Shiner closely.

"Just give him back to me," I repeated.

The man gave me a little shove to the chest. "Listen, kid, you ain't very friendly. I just want to see him, that's all. I ain't going to hurt him."

Looking up, I saw Shiner starting to get mad. He stood up on his hind legs, pawing the air.

"I just think you'd better give him back to me. I don't think he likes being on your shoulder, that's all."

"Oh, I see," the man said, puffing the big cigar. "I tell you what. I'll give him back to you when I'm good and ready, and right now I ain't ready."

I looked over at Troop, shaking my head. I could tell Troop wanted to help but didn't know what to do.

The big man scooted Shiner up to the top of his head with his thick fat hand. "Hey, everyone," he shouted, "look at my coonskin cap!"

Everyone doubled over laughing except for Troop and me. Shiner didn't think it was one bit funny either.

The man strutted back and forth, giving Shiner a hard time balancing himself on his head. He chattered and the man laughed and shouted. All at once, Shiner burrowed his head into the thick thatch of dark curls on the man's head. His sharp claws pawed the man's scalp and he took a mouthful of hair in his teeth, pulling like everything. The man's hands went up. He screeched so loud everyone on the midway turned around to see what was going on. He tried getting Shiner off, and when he couldn't, he raced up and down screaming and screeching, his arms flying everywhere. Now everyone really had a big laugh.

136

Some were laughing so hard they toppled over to the ground, holding their sides. Troop and I stayed sober. We just wanted the whole thing to end so we could get Shiner back and get out of there.

Finally, he grabbed Shiner by the scruff of his neck and pulled him off, scowling like crazy. I held my breath, not knowing what he was planning to do next. I got ready to run in and defend Shiner, but I guess I didn't have to worry; Shiner took care of himself. He turned his head and buried his needle-sharp teeth in that big man's fat hand. Instantly, the man dropped Shiner to the ground, screaming and cussing. Shiner took off like a rabbit. Troop and I were right behind him. In the distance, we heard the big man shouting angrily and the crowd still roaring with laughter.

When we caught up with Shiner, he was crouched beneath a tent shaking with fright. I lifted him up, smoothed his fur and tried to calm him. Troop looked at him with serious eyes. I knew he had something on his mind. His face looked real sober, almost a frown.

I nuzzled Shiner lovingly, and his body shook. "There...there, old boy. You're okay," I said. "That big hulk isn't going to bother you any more." I looked over at Troop. He was still frowning. I couldn't stand it any longer. I had to know. "What is it, Troop? I know that look on your face. You've got something on your mind. What is it?"

Troop hunched his shoulders and looked away. He didn't want to say anything. I continued petting Shiner. I saw the back of Troop's head with his long hair falling from his hat. "Troop," I said, "we're best friends, ain't we? Remember two years ago, when we cut our thumbs and became blood brothers? We both belong to the Mustangs. We've been through a lot together. We've always been honest with each other, that's for sure. If you've got something to say, I want you to say it."

Troop looked around. His eyes burned through me. "I'm worried about Shiner, Carley," he said. "Real worried."

"What are you talking about?" I asked, cradling Shiner in my arms.

"He's not the same, Carley. Ever since we got him out of the tree at the river, he's been different."

I looked up. "What're you talking about?"

"He's just different, that's all. Sometimes he's wild as a bobcat and sometimes he's just as lazy as can be. He goes from one thing to another."

I stood there not saying a word. I didn't know what Troop was getting at.

"You remember that day we found him. I told you then that I didn't believe in penning wild animals up. They were meant to stay in nature. Manito gave them instincts. They must return to the wild."

I stepped back.

Troop went on: "We've both seen Shiner wild, and we've both seen him just laying around when we're fishing. He's been in your Ma's flour bin, ruining the whole kitchen, and he's been on top of your outdoor toilet causing your Pa all kinds of trouble. Even the way he acted today with that man wasn't like him. Scratching and biting and all. It just wasn't like him, that's all. You told me sometimes he just stands up on his hind legs against the screen looking out into the night as though he's looking for something."

I nodded. Troop was acting too serious for my own comfort.

"Something's happening to him, Carley. Shiner is growing up."

"What does that mean?" I asked bitterly.

Troop stuck a blade of grass between his teeth and sat crosslegged on the ground. He pulled off his hat, letting the breeze blow his hair back from his forehead. "Think what we saw in that tree that day. Think hard."

138

"Well," I said, "we saw Shiner and another coon. Just another coon, that's all." My throat was dry.

"Not just another coon...a female coon, I think. And, I think Shiner's instincts are telling him something. I think they're telling him to go back to the wild to choose a mate."

I looked at Troop and then down at Shiner. I pulled him closer to me. The sound of the calliope, the intermingling smells of hot dogs, cotton candy, and pickled pigs feet all left me. I only thought of what Troop was saying and the meaning behind it. "I hope you don't mean what I think you mean," I said.

"I know animals, Carley. You've always said that. In fact, you always said Indians must be half-animal since we understand them so well."

I couldn't deny that. Doggone that Troop. Did he always have to make so much sense? I asked myself.

"What I see, and I'll bet almost everyone would agree, is that here's an animal needing to go back to the wild real bad. He's finding out that he doesn't fit here any more. That's why he's so unsettled, so jumpy. One minute he just lays around hardly moving and the next he's all excitable, causing all kinds of trouble."

I shook my head. "Well, I'm not taking him back," I said stubbornly. "You can count on that. He's my pet. He's my friend. We do everything together. We play together, even sleep together. Where I go, Shiner goes. We're buddies."

Troop nodded his head. Boosting himself up, he brushed the dust off his backside, then put on his hat. He walked over to me and stroked Shiner. "Okay, Carley, you win. Maybe I'm wrong. Maybe Shiner will be fine."

I looked up into his eyes. A shiver raced down my back and I drew Shiner closer to me.

"Oh, come on, let's forget about this," I said. "I want to go see if my cucumber won anything and to see if Ma took any ribbons." I shook my head. "If she didn't, those judges don't know anything about good cooking; that's for sure."

People milled tightly about in the tent. Shiner perched on my shoulder, standing on his hind legs and stretching to see. People bumped into each other along the lines, watching the judging of the baked goods.

"Come on, Troop," I whispered. "Let's nudge our way closer. I want to see if Ma's baked goods get anything."

Troop nodded. We bumped and elbowed our way through the crowd until we stood right smack dab in front of the long display of tables. I spotted Ma's breads, pies and cakes among the others immediately. You could tell them a mile away. They were the best looking ones there. Four judges were passing by, sampling each and every one of the baked products. There were two men and two women. I would've liked that job, that's for sure. Except maybe until I went to bed, probably with the worst case of stomach cramps in history. Kind of like the time I ate a dozen harvest apples and thought I was going to die for sure.

"That's Ma's stuff down there," I said, pointing down the long row of tables. "Look at those pies and cakes." My mouth watered. Ma, standing down the table from us, caught my eye and raised her hand with her fingers crossed. I gave her the same sign, and Troop did, too.

The four judges stood in front of Troop and me, tasting small cuts of pies and cakes. The ladies had big fancy hats with feathers, flowers, and veils. They took tiny bites, chewing with their eyes closed. I guess they could think better by closing their eyes. The men, both in their Sunday best, took bigger bites, rolling their eyes back into their heads, savoring the taste. It was plum crazy watching them. Every eye in the crowded tent was on their wagging jaws.

Shiner stood on my shoulder chattering. He moved

about restlessly. I didn't want to leave until I found out if Ma won or if I got a ribbon for my four-pound cucumber.

Setting on the long tables was a feast fit for a king. There was so much sweet stuff it made my teeth ache: pies of all sorts, some with crusts, others with meringue— apple, peach, cherry, raisin, chocolate, strawberry, banana, custard, cream, butterscotch, and coconut. And there were cakes with big gooey waves of frosting: chocolate, vanilla, applesauce, rum, bundt, angel food, and a whole lot of others. Cakes with nuts and coconut. Cakes topped with cherries. Cakes with fancy frosting designs.

Further down were jars of pickles, beets, peaches, pears, tomatoes, beans, and peas, all setting proud in mason jars, the glass sparkling clean. And still further down were rolls, both sweet and plain.

Shiner shifted on my shoulder. I petted his head. "Be still, boy. We'll go in just a little while. The judges are just about to Ma's cakes now."

Troop looked worriedly up at Shiner.

People clapped as different entries won. A white, red, blue, or purple ribbon was tacked on the article. Ladies placed their fingers over their lips daintily when their names were called out as winners and recognized with applause.

One lady judge, with a big ostrich feather sticking out of her hat, tasted a thin slice of Ma's cake. She stood back, closing her eyes while chewing. Ma made those X's with her fingers again. I knew how much this meant to her.

Just as the lady with the feather smiled, opened her eyes and fished a purple ribbon out of her box, I felt my shoulder get a whole lot lighter. Shiner leaped right down in the middle of Ma's three layer chocolate supreme cake. I made a wild grab for him as he sat smack dab in the cake. He dodged my hand, leaping out of there right into a big banana pie with a mountain of meringue. From there, he went from one baked good to another, prancing and jumping in them. Ladies screamed, men bellowed, grabbing for him. Kids laughed, beating each other on the backs.

"A wild raccoon!" someone shouted.

"Maybe it has rabies!" another cried.

Everyone was hollering and screaming wildly as Shiner ran along the whole length of that big display, jumping in cakes and pies and knocking off canned vegetables and jams.

The lady judge with the feather fainted and the man judge waved something strong smelling beneath her nose. Her hat slid over her eyes. She was out like a light.

Pickles and jellies crashed to the floor. Pies, cakes, and breads fell to the floor or were ruined as Shiner raced back and forth, trying to stay out of reach of groping hands.

A sick ball formed in my stomach. I hoped I'd wake up soon and all of this would be just a nightmare. I'd be all sweaty and clammy like I was when I dreamed about monsters, but I'd be safe in my bed and the moonlight would be flowing right through my window. My old bed and dresser would be there. My baseball glove, model planes, and dirty clothes on the floor would be there. Shiner would be there laying across my chest, sleeping like a baby.

But, this wasn't a dream. This was for real and it was happening right now. I didn't have time to look at the stark horror on Ma's face since I was so busy trying to get hold of Shiner. He jumped, rolled, hopped, leaped, ran, and somersaulted as fast as he could. He jumped from the table and ran into the crowd between people's legs. Ladies hollered, moving clear back. One fat lady crawled on a table. She stood there on all fours while the table wobbled back and forth. Finally, it gave way, spilling her and the rest of the baked goods to the ground.

Shiner hopped and jumped from shoulders to heads. Men yelled, women screamed, kids laughed and cried. There was so much noise going on in the tent that a body just couldn't think straight.

A siren sounded outside. People parted, making an aisle for Sheriff Parsons and his deputy. The deputy clutched a net in his hand. I knew it was the same one used for stray and mad dogs. My heart fell to the bottom of my feet.

Shiner scrambled up the tent poles, peering down and chattering at the people looking up at him. Then he made a big leap to the ground. The net flew over him and he was thrown into a cage. The door snapped shut and was locked. I ran over and knelt down, pulling on the door. It wouldn't budge. Shiner looked up at me through the wire mesh. I knew there were tears in those black eyes of his. I could tell that he was real sorry, but he had no control over himself.

Troop and I stood there as Sheriff Parsons and his deputy carried the cage out to their car. The engine roared, the siren blasted, and Shiner was gone.

I felt empty inside. I didn't notice the broken glass, spilled cakes, pies, jams, jellies, breads and rolls all over the ground. I never noticed the purple ribbon tacked to my four-pound cucumber. The only thing I knew was that Shiner was gone. Troop had been dead right about him.

Chapter 13

"School starts day after tomorrow," Troop said, pulling a blade of grass through his teeth.

"This summer's gone like a streak," I replied, looking up at a row of puffy-like clouds. "I can tell because you don't see as many fire flies. And a night or two ago I had to get up and get a blanket out of the closet to put on my bed. That's always a sure sign of summer being over."

"It's been a good summer," Troop said. "My pa has worked all summer. My ma has your ma for a friend, and she's learning a little English."

"My ma likes your ma, Troop. They're friends just like we are now."

"Yeah. I know your ma taught her to make a real good triple layer supreme chocolate cake." He licked his lips. "Ummmm-mmm, boy, that was good."

"And your ma taught my ma to make hoe cakes and what herbs to use for spices and medicines."

Troop lay there, his head cushioned on his arm, his hat tipped over his eyes, the sun on his bare chest. He was waiting for the last of the summer's bullheads to bite. "It's been exciting, too," he continued. "Climbing Cave Springs Mountain, Darrell's initiation, Luke Webster shooting up the town and then his great miracle. All of that..."

Pushing my hat back with a thumb, I turned my head toward Troop. "Indians are good at a lot of things, but one thing they aren't good at is trying to keep from talking about things on their mind," I said.

Troop bumped his hat away from his forehead and stared at me. "What are you talking about, Carley?"

"You mentioned everything that happened to us this summer. Everything, but one thing."

Troop looked away. "I didn't want to remind you, that's all."

My face got red-hot. I can't remember when I was ever mad at Troop. Troop and I had always been the best of friends. We never got mad at each other. "You talked about everything except Shiner!" My teeth gritted together. "Don't you know I think about him all the time there in that cage?"

Troop nodded sadly. "I know you do, Carley. I'm sorry. I just didn't want to make you feel bad, that's all."

I felt ashamed down to my toes. I should've known Troop was doing it for my own good. He was that kind of friend.

"What are you going to do about it?" he asked.

I hunched my shoulders. "I don't know. All I know is that it almost makes me sick thinking of him there in that cage. I've got to do something."

"Sheriff Parsons' mind is pretty much set. He thinks Shiner went crazy." Troop bowed his head. "I don't know what they've got planned for him."

I looked up, seeing fear in Troop's eyes. "You don't think they're planning to kill him, do you?" I asked.

"I don't want to say. But the Sheriff did say he was a menace and couldn't be allowed to stay in town. You heard that part."

"Yeah, I know," I said dejectedly. "I know Ma and Pa don't want me to have him any more either after what happened at the fair."

"Your Ma was pretty mad, wasn't she?"

"Sure, and who could blame her? Shiner ruined the whole display. Everybody's entries were ruined. One lady fainted. People were scared out of their wits. There were pies, cakes, broken jars...everything all over the ground. Pa probably lost some customers over what happened. I can't blame either of them for being real mad at him. They gave him plenty of chances. He just messed them up, that's all."

"How much time do you have, Carley?"

"Sheriff Parsons told Pa that they would make a decision by the end of the week. That's tomorrow."

"You can't let them do that. You just can't sit here fishing and wait for them to..." Troop looked away.

"Why don't you go ahead and say it? Until they kill him. That's what they're planning on doing." A lump jumped into my throat and I choked.

Troop looked at me helplessly.

I laid back on the ground, putting my arm across my eyes. No way was I going to let Troop see tears running down my face. "I know one thing, Troop, if I listened to you, none of this would've happened. You were dead right. Shiner's instincts to return to the wild and mate were plain as day. I was too stubborn to see it. Or maybe I didn't want to see it. I knew if I faced it, he'd have to leave and I sure didn't want that. I wanted Shiner for a pet forever. I should've listened to you. You tried to tell me."

"For once, I wish I wasn't right. I really do," Troop said solemnly.

Wiping the tears away, I sat up. "I'm not going to let it happen, that's all."

"Not let what happen?" Troop asked.

"I'm not going to let the Sheriff kill Shiner. Shiner's just acting like he's supposed to act. It's his instincts telling him to go back to the wild. He's not mad and he doesn't have rabies. He's as normal as can be." Balling my hands into fists, I jumped to my feet. "Come on, let's do something about this instead of laying around blubbering about it."

Troop jumped to his feet as well. "What're you planning to do?" he asked.

"Come on," I said, pulling my line out of the water. "Let's go talk to Sheriff Parsons."

Sheriff Parsons twirled his handle bar mustache in thought. "I just don't know how I can let you boys take him. He really caused havoc at the fair the other day. This animal is a threat and a menace. He could hurt someone."

Kneeling down, I looked at Shiner nervously pacing back and forth in the little wire cage. I never saw him look more pitiful. He looked worse than when he was in the trap. He was skinny and his eyes were wet around them like he had done a whole lot of crying. I didn't know if animals cry when they're sad, but I don't know why they wouldn't. They have feelings just like people.

I looked up at the Sheriff. "Please, Sheriff, Shiner was just telling us in the only way he knew that it was time for him to go back to nature. It was time for him to mate and live like a raccoon should back in the woods. I was too dumb to realize it." I nodded toward Troop. "Troop tried to tell me. I never wanted him to leave. He's the best friend a kid could have."

Sheriff Parsons shook his head. "You boys are putting me in a real spot. I have a duty to the people of Belford. They voted me in this job to protect them and that's what I intend to do."

I didn't want to ask it, but I knew I had to. "What are you going to do to him tomorrow, Sheriff?"

Sheriff Parsons looked away. I knew he wasn't a mean man. In fact, he was a nice man. He always helped old people and kids. He was always friendly to everybody. I knew he was only doing what he thought was his duty.

"Now, Carley Bimberg, I wish you wouldn't ask me such a question. Besides, I think you know the answer. I've already told your Pa. I'll have to..." He wagged his head. "Well, you know."

I looked up, my eyes filling with tears. "Kill him! That's what you're trying to say, isn't it? Tomorrow, you're going to kill Shiner!"

Troop's head bowed on his chest.

"I'm sorry, Carley," the Sheriff said. "It just has to be done. I can't take any chances on Shiner hurting anyone. I wish I didn't have to do it."

I fingered Shiner's wet nose through the wire. My heart went out to him. I wished I had returned him to the wild just as soon as we got him out of the trap. His eyes looked up at me for help. I knew I had to do something. I didn't know what, but I knew I had to do something.

The telephone rang in the Sheriff's office. He looked soberly at Shiner and then at me. "I'm real sorry, boys. There's just no other way. I'm real sorry."

The phone rang again. Sheriff Parsons looked toward his office. He sighed deeply. "Sorry, boys, I'll be right back. I've got to answer that. Deputy Carter is out this morning."

Troop and I nodded sadly.

Sheriff Parsons left the back room to answer the phone. We heard his voice talking to a woman who was having trouble getting her cat out of a tree.

I looked at Shiner. Then I looked at Troop. Our eyes met. Those black eyes of his burned a hole through me. We knew each other so long that both of us instantly knew what we had to do.

I looked about the room for the key. Troop spotted it first, hanging from a hook on the wall. Reaching up, he grabbed it and handed it to me. I hurriedly unlocked the padlock, looking warily over my shoulder to the Sheriff's office.

Swinging open the cage door, Shiner sprang out and ran up my arm to perch on my shoulder. We could still hear the Sheriff talking to the woman about her cat in the tree. I nodded at Troop and carefully we tiptoed out the back door with Shiner balanced on my right shoulder. Once we got out into the alley, we ran like we were being chased by a pack of wolves.

Chapter 14

Troop and I stayed off the road, walking through tall grass in the culverts. We couldn't take the chance of being seen. Weeds beat us in the face and got down our necks, making us feel itchy. We swiped back rows and rows of bright sunflowers.

Sweat dripped off my face in streams. Shiner chattered excitedly on my shoulder. I tried hushing him, but it didn't do any good. Shiner knew he was free and he was expressing his happiness. We walked two miles through those weeds, thistles, and sunflowers. Although it was the first part of September, it was still hot, and the sun was bearing down on both of us.

Troop peeked through the weeds. "Get down!" he yelled. "Here comes the Sheriff's car. Drop down!"

Without a word, I fell on my belly. Shiner, acting as if he realized the danger, crouched down beneath my arm. We laid there, quiet-like, hearing the car's tires grating the rocks beneath its wheels as it slowly passed by. We started breathing again when the car passed us. Troop took off his hat and wiped the sweat from his brow.

"Whew! That was close!"

"Yeah, it sure was," I replied. "I feel like a criminal or something."

"Yeah, I know what you mean," Troop said. "I suppose we're in real trouble."

I looked at Troop. I felt guilty as heck. "You shouldn't be in on this. This is my concern. Shiner is my pet. You shouldn't have to be in any trouble over this." I pointed down the road. "Why don't you go on back and say it was all my doing? It's not right for you to get into trouble over this."

Troop looked back at me through piercing eyes. "I thought we were blood brothers, Carley. Blood brothers stick together no matter what. Besides, I don't want anything bad to happen to Shiner either."

My throat got clogged up, and I had trouble speaking. "You're a real good friend, Troop, and that's for sure." Reaching out, I squeezed his shoulder. I knew that if I lived to be a hundred, I'd never find a friend as good as Troop Whitewater.

"We'd better go now, Carley," Troop said. "The Sheriff could find us any moment. We'd better hurry and get to the bridge before he comes back."

I nodded, picking up Shiner and placed him on my shoulder. We continued walking through the towering weeds.

After an hour, the rush of water came to our ears. We were getting close to the river bridge. It didn't seem possible that the water was down and running slow when only a few weeks ago it was rushing in a rampage.

"We can run down this bank, Carley. That'll give us a short cut." Troop parted the weeds.

I saw the muddy Blue River snaking its way along the banks. We were about a half mile from the bridge.

We raced down the steep bank, slipping and sliding, getting coated with mud on our legs and backsides.

"Hurry, Carley! Hurry!" Troop hollered over his shoulder.

I ran breathlessly, feeling Shiner bounce all over my shoulder, clinging as tight as he could.

Once we got to the bottom, we ran along the bank next to the water. Driftwood branches, and fallen logs were scattered along the bank. We hurtled them and kept on running. We had to find just the right place to let Shiner go.

Sweat ran down my face and back. I was breathing so hard I was gasping. Even Troop, who never had trouble running, was getting tired. When he gets tired, you know it must be a hard run.

I tripped and fell down on the bank, breathing hard and feeling too weak to get up. Glancing over my shoulder, my heart fell to the bottom of my feet. There on the bridge, shouting his lungs out and waving his hands, was Sheriff Parsons. Troop looked at me.

Without saying another word, we jumped to our feet and ran for all we were worth. We looked behind us, seeing the Sheriff racing down the bank next to the bridge, coming toward us.

As I ran, thoughts swept through my mind. I couldn't believe I was doing this. I was actually running from the law. I could imagine what Ma and Pa would say if they could see me now. I knew I'd have to go to bed right after supper until I was old enough to grow a beard. I probably wouldn't get any allowance until I was twenty-one. I wouldn't get to listen to the radio for at least ten years. Maybe I'd even go to jail, breaking the law like this. A cold shiver darted down my back as I thought of Luke Webster in that jail cell months ago. In the distance, I heard the Sheriff shouting.

Troop and I kept on running, jumping logs and drift wood along the river bank.

"Should we give ourselves up, Troop?" I shouted. "Sheriff Parsons is only about a half mile behind us now. We're in a whole lot of trouble. Maybe we can save ourselves if we stop right now and let him catch us," I gasped.

Troop shook his head. "No, Carley," he said out of breath. "If we do, you know what will happen to Shiner. We've got to keep going until we get to the woods. It's the only way."

I nodded. Troop was right. There was no other way. We would have to take our punishment later, that's all. I was right on Troop's heels, looking at that long black hair flying in the breeze.

Sheriff Parsons shouted, ordering us to halt, but we didn't. Shiner managed to stay balanced on my shoulder even though I was running like heck. I couldn't believe how he could do that. Ten minutes later, I knew I couldn't run one more step. I stumbled, dropping to the ground. "Troop...Troop..." I gasped, "I've got to stop. I can't go one step more. This has to be it."

Troop stopped and walked back to where I was sitting. He looked in the distance at the Sheriff running toward us, his fist in the air.

"All right, Carley, I guess this has to be it."

I carefully took Shiner off my shoulder. He looked up at me. His eyes told me he knew that an important decision had been made. I nuzzled his fur lovingly. Troop walked over, petted him and said nothing. His eyes told me that I had to do something quick or it would be too late.

"Shiner," I said, "I'm setting you free. You've been a real good friend this whole summer, but it's time now for you to go back to nature. Ever since we took you out of that tree during the flood, you've been trying to tell me that this is where you belong. Now, I see that this is the right place for you." I nuzzled his furry face once more. He chattered at me.

I placed him on the ground. "Go ahead, Shiner," I said. "You've got to run right now. The Sheriff is coming for you. You've got to go right now!"

Shiner looked up at me. He stood upon his hind legs and looked around at the slow moving river and the tall trees and the muddy river banks. He seemed to know that this is where he belonged and at last he had returned. My throat closed and I had trouble speaking. "Go ahead, boy. Go ahead, and have a real good life."

Shiner ran a few steps and stopped, then turned and looked me right in the eyes as if to make sure that this was what I wanted. I nodded my head, motioning for him to hurry.

154

Sheriff Parsons was so close I felt the vibration of his heavy feet on the bank. "Hurry, Shiner! Hurry! Run for your life!" I yelled.

Shiner dropped to all fours and ran toward the woods. I watched him weave in and out around the logs and driftwood. My eyes lost him and then picked him up again coming out of the weeds. Just before he disappeared in the thick wooded area, another raccoon crawled down out of a tree, racing toward him. It was a female, I was sure. Shiner was home and everything was right. My vision blurred with tears as both raccoons disappeared into the weeds.

Sheriff Parsons ran up next to Troop and me. His face was beet-red and he was breathing so hard he couldn't talk for several moments. At last, he caught his breath. "You boys could be in real trouble," he said, gasping.

Wiping away the tears that were racing down my cheeks, I looked up and smiled at him. "I know, Sheriff. We're ready to take our medicine. We had no right doing what we did. It's just that we couldn't wait and have you kill him. This is where Shiner belongs. He's not mad, and he doesn't have rabies. He was trying to tell us that he needed to go back to the wild. His instincts were telling us that, and he just couldn't control himself." I poked my chest. "It's my fault. Troop tried to tell me that he needed to go back, but I just wouldn't listen." I hung my head, feeling ashamed. "I'm sorry, Sheriff. We'll both go back with you in the police car and take our medicine." Troop walked over and stood beside me.

The Sheriff, now catching his breath, sighed. He looked into the distance at the wooded area where Shiner and the female raccoon disappeared, cleared his throat and hunched his shoulders. "Heck," he said, "I suppose I would've done the same thing if I loved my pet as much as you boys. Besides, I guess there's no danger to anyone now that he's back in the wilderness. He's back where he belongs."

I looked up. "You mean it's all right? You mean you aren't going to arrest us?"

Sheriff Parsons shook his head. "I'm not saying what you did was right." He petted his handle bar mustache. "In fact, it was very wrong. The only thing I'm saying is that I understand. And as long as Shiner is here where he belongs, he can't be a threat or menace, can he?" He smiled, pulling at the brim of his hat.

"Right, Sheriff! Right!" I exclaimed.

Troop grinned, slapping me on the back with relief.

Sheriff Parsons shook his head this time with a smile. "I tell you what. I'll give you boys a ride back in the police car. That's a mighty long trip back, and you both look as if you could use a lift."

Troop and I nodded at once.

The Sheriff, Troop, and I started back toward the bridge. Once, on a ridge, I stopped and looked back. The woods were thick and green—and home, to Shiner. I wasn't happy, yet I really wasn't sad either. Shiner had been my pet for over three months, and he had been a good friend. Now he was free, and I hoped he'd be happy.

THE END